THE INCORPORATION OF ERIC CHUNG

STEVEN C. LO

THE INCORPORATION OF
ERIC CHUNG

小說

A NOVEL

ALGONQUIN BOOKS OF CHAPEL HILL
1989

Published by
Algonquin Books of Chapel Hill
Post Office Box 2225
Chapel Hill, North Carolina 27515-2225
a division of
Workman Publishing Company
708 Broadway
New York, New York 10003

Design by Molly Renda
Jacket illustration by Mike Quon

LIBRARY OF CONGRESS CATALOGING-IN-PUBLICATION DATA

Lo, Steven C.
The Incorporation of Eric Chung: a novel/by Steven C. Lo. — 1st ed.
p.   cm.
ISBN 0-945575-18-1
I. Title.
PS3562.016D45   1989
813'.54—dc20   89-6763
CIP

10 9 8 7 6 5 4 3 2 1

FIRST EDITION

To my father, Tsu-Zun Lo, a subject of imperial Japan at birth, a Chinese national at age thirty-four, and in 1989, at age seventy-eight, a U.S. citizen.

CONTENTS

THE INCORPORATION OF ERIC CHUNG

1. TO START WITH

TO START WITH, I WANT to make it clear about what I'm going to say. I'd like to go into this without a lot of misunderstanding, if I can. I don't mean to imply that what I will say is so complicated that if I don't spell it out for you in the first place you will end up getting it all wrong. It isn't and you won't. What I mean is people do expect a lot, you know, sometimes. And I don't want anybody getting excited, at any time, thinking I am going into a great romance or drama or even something important here. I am not and that's too much responsibility. To start with.

The only thing I'm going to say is about my current situation. That's pretty much it, more or less. Sure I'll get into the background and the past and all that and end up telling you a great deal of what you might call "unrelated" things—in fair amount of details too. But it's only to explain, the only way I know, that, in the final analysis, everything that happened happened because it made perfectly good common sense. Nothing came out of the blue. Nothing was evil, corrupt, or diabolic enough to make the blood boil. No heroes either. No one tried to be one, not that there was any need.

Come to think of it, there isn't any part of what I'm going to say, *any* part, that would get in your local paper even if I hired a PR man. This is not the kind of stuff that gets you to drop your sports pages, I have to admit. Definitely not movie material either. It does concern me a lot, though, at least in the past few months, and I think it concerns Mary, my secretary. That's all—and I have to assume the part about Mary being concerned. Otherwise, I can't think of any reasons, by any stretch of imagination, why it should concern someone else. Absolutely no reasons. Now, I understand this makes the whole deal sound kind of silly and mundane, but that's all I have to say now. Granted, I may think of other things to say some other time, but that's some other time.

In fact, to be businesslike about it, I can "telegraph" you this entire thing in less than a page. Like I used to do, a lot, when I worked at Taltex Electronics. There was a rule that forbade memos longer than one page—this was at Taltex. Secretaries could not type or hand out memos longer than one page, or *even they* would have "severe probationary measures" put on them. The company could really get nasty on this kind of thing. Employees actually vied with each other to be "concise and telegraphic" with their office messages. And the same rule also said you had to write most everything down for the record. So when people were hired, they were told on the first day, among other things, to "always memo it" and "always telegraph." It did get out of hand once in a while with some smart aleck sending BULL SHIT! on one entire page to our office in Singapore or somewhere. But in general, it was a good rule. I liked it a lot. I didn't have much to say then, almost ten years ago, as a Systems Programmer/Analyst One. And even if I did, I could never, *ever*, have come up with enough words to fill a whole page anyway.

English hadn't become *easy* for me at the time (to my great disappointment), despite it was already my fifth year here in the States. And there was no telling when it was *going to*. I did treat the memos seriously though, giving them my hard labor, sometimes spending two, three mornings on one, making corrections on the verbs, and many other things, so that they would not read like bad translations from something of my own language. I kept a dictionary and a grammar book in the office, on top of my computer monitor. I always proofread. I often looked up new words, words like "alacrity" or "concentrical," and during lunch hours planned various ways of using them in a sentence. My memos still came out very short, averaging a quarter page or less, and all had embarrassing mistakes.

Anyway, my current situation, telegraphed, would be: COLDWELL COMPANY EXECUTIVE, ERIC CHUNG, REMOVED FROM JOB, STRIPPED OF DUTIES, SOON TO BE CANNED. There. Fifteen words, twenty if you count the punctuation. If I really want to do it, I can take away my name, for obvious reasons, and erase STRIPPED OF DUTIES because it kind of follows REMOVED FROM JOB anywhere you go. So now you have COLDWELL COMPANY EXECUTIVE REMOVED FROM JOB/SOON TO BE CANNED. Ten words. Period. The entire story. I am not saying I won't make it more interesting—I will try—but that's pretty much it. No more, no less. I am keeping things brief. You'd do the same if English had been as tough for you.

2. (SEE BACK)

THIS IS AS GOOD A PLACE as any to go into a report of my past. History—and I mean personal history—can be a lot more important than people think. Sometimes you can't even begin to talk about your problems if you don't first explain your past. *That* I should know. *That* I came to appreciate often—more often than I wanted—by standing in a four-hour-long line in front of the Federal Building, waiting in hot sun or cold wind with my fellow "aliens," filling out forms as we inched along, hoping in the end to have a five-minute conference with an officer at the Immigration (by the three o'clock quitting time). It was a process I had to repeat several times a year for about ten years, thanks to the immigration laws, in order to keep being "documented" and "registered." Each time the line seemed longer.

The forms in our hands had to be in perfect order when we finally reached the windows, behind which the immigration officers sat. Particularly, the "Personal History" section of the form should be well filled out. This was the part that started all forms (and there were many forms, each with a specific purpose), and it had the tiniest spaces to write in and asked for plenty of "exact dates," "exact street addresses," and so on. You knew you had done well on this section when you had accounted for every single day of your life since your "Date of Entry into U. S." Anything less would surely fail to bring out the enthusiasm in the officers. People were known to have been sent back to the end of the line for defiantly leaving the entire section blank.

On every visit, I provided my history as required in the smallest and neatest print I could manage. I learned, through word of mouth and experience, that it was permitted to write "See Back" in those tiny spaces and continue the reports on extra blank sheets. (And I always had such sheets with me.) My past always read organized, factual, and consistent. I also learned to end my report exactly on my Date of Entry. No part of my life in my old country was of interest to the officers.

Before I became the President of Coldwell Electronics International, Inc.—the job I am about to lose—I was the Special Advisor of the same company (See Back). Before that I was the Manager of China Affairs, also at Coldwell Electronics International, Inc., a division of Coldwell Enterprises (See Back). Before that I worked at Taltex as System Programmer/Analyst for two and a half years. Before that I worked in a small company in Lubbock as a Computer Operator, first the night, then the regular shift. Before that I was at Texas Tech University Graduate School; there I worked in several part-time jobs. These part-time jobs bordered on "unlawful employment" because I had never obtained work papers. Still, on the many forms at the Immigration, I reported them with good amount of honest details. No one I knew had successfully deceived a U. S. immigration officer. No one should have tried.

•   •   •

5

The last part-time job I held was in the Texas Tech library as a Stack Control Assistant. The job was, according to my superior, the Stack Control Manager, "simply putting the books back correctly." "Putting the books back" meant to get books, already sorted and loaded on small wheeled carts, from the Stack Control Area and return them to the shelves. "Correctly" meant the books should only go back to their "precise alphanumeric positions," or else. "A 'mis-shelved' book is a lost book" was the motto for me and a small army of Outbound SCAs (Stack Control Assistants). The Inbound SCAs, also a small army working in the Stack Control Area, sorting the books and loading the carts, had their own motto, which did not concern us. They, the Inbound SCAs, came out once in a while to retrieve "*dis*-shelved" books, but mostly they milled about in a big room. Outbound SCAs, on the other hand, had to put in genuine labor: we had to reach up and down the shelves.

When the entire student body crowded the library for the finals, things got hairy with people scattering books all over the place. The Inbound SCAs came out more often and quickly cleaned up. But for us, the Outbound SCAs, who could only shelve so many books at a time, the sudden surge was a plain disaster. More and more books were left in the Stack Control Area. The Stack Control Manager complained: "Look at all this." He stood, facing us, before a long row of fully loaded carts. "We need to get these back in circulation, you know." The Stack Control Manager seldom picked on us, unless the Assistant Librarian had been on his case. We could see the Inbound SCAs smirking behind him, showing deep contempt for us.

So we charged ourselves up and shelved more than ever. But, every time we turned around, more loaded carts awaited us.

Inbound SCAs now became our biggest enemies. All of us were frustrated, angry, and suffering from back pains. The Stack Control Manager even hinted that we might be goofing off. "I'll show you how you can shelve four carts an hour," he announced. The industry average was two carts an hour then. So he pushed out four carts and, in an hour, emptied all of them. He got another four, and sure enough, all books were gone quickly. We couldn't believe it. This guy must have known "alphanumerics" like the back of his hand.

By the time he got to his third round, several of us had decided it was imperative to learn how he did it. So we stopped the work and secretly followed him. We saw him push a cart to a convenient spot. He glanced at the book codes, skillfully shelved a few books like the bunch of us would, then, to our amazement, he began throwing the books on the desks, chairs, and even the floor between the shelves. The first cart was emptied out just like that. The second cart was no different. Neither was the third and the fourth. Everyone was *astounded*. But we were, being intelligent college students, also enlightened.

After this small lesson from the Stack Control Manager, our shelving speed quickly improved. From two to four carts an hour. Then to five. A few of us even got carried away and did six an hour—unheard of among the nation's major libraries. The joke was now squarely on the Inbound SCAs. But as far as the Stack Control Manager and the Assistant Librarian were concerned, the "circulation" was better than good, it was fabulous. And the one thing I learned from the job, other than you must pay the taxes regardless of how little you make, was that it's important to have others, especially your bosses, think you are doing well. Whatever *you* really think is sometimes best kept to yourself.

Before the library job I was a pot scrubber and then a waiter at a sorority house on campus. I was a pot scrubber much longer than a waiter. As a pot scrubber I had to deal with pots and pans only, leaving the dishes and glasses to the dishwasher, a sophomore. And the waiters, mostly seniors, served food in ties and uniforms. I was content with scrubbing the identical set of pots and pans twice a day until one day the housemother promoted me past the dishwasher to a waiter. She immediately saw her terrible mistake when a girl asked for salad dressing and had to describe it for me. The housemother was still nice and all that, but I didn't think the sorority house was right for me anymore. They only paid in free meals anyway.

Before that I worked for a wealthy family in Lubbock doing odd jobs like raking leaves, carving the Thanksgiving turkey, and so on. I always made a point to dress in my best shirts, one of them embroidered silk, when I had to work in the house. The lady of the house was pleased with that. She soon had me standing by, in the living area, when she entertained. I'd only stand there, looking like a butler, taking orders from the lady and her guests, and I'd pass the chores to people in the kitchen who did the real work. The better I dressed the more tips I got from her, and the less I had to do.

The lady often hired student help for her parties. Once she had a married couple and me, all from the Graduate School, working a small banquet. I was in my usual white shirt and black slacks, perfectly ironed. The couple arrived in jeans and T-shirts. The husband, sensitive enough to have noticed the difference, murmured, "I think I should've put on a white shirt."

"Nah," the wife objected, "you look just great, honey." She ignored my friendly greeting.

That night I looked handsome and helpful beside the lady of the house while the couple chopped celeries, washed dishes, and mopped the kitchen floor, and, I was sure, got paid less than I.

Before that was a summer job in Albany, New York, as a life-guard at a swimming pool in a motel. From Lubbock, I drove four and a half days to upper state New York with a couple of other foreign students. We had been told that summer jobs were easy to find there and that if we chose to go to places like Los Angeles, Houston, or Las Vegas, we wouldn't see "real America." I got a deep tan, and was happy my life-saving skills, which involved the use of a long steel rod provided by the motel, were never called upon.

Before that I worked in a dog training school in Lubbock for three days as a dog washer. I quit because I was very sure one of the dogs was going to kill me.

Before that I was a bartender at Hillcrest Country Club of Lubbock. The woman manager of the club had been depressed by her inability to find a bartender for three months when I happened to come by. "I don't care," she said to me, "if you are black or white or red or . . . " She stopped.

"Chinese," I disclosed.

"Chinese, yeah, I don't care," she blurted. "You want the job, you got it."

Most of the drinks were not difficult for an apprentice bar-tender. West Texas gentlemen liked drinks with self-explanatory names: rum and Coke, Scotch and water, for example. Those who got smart and threw out things like Singapore Sling would end up making the drinks themselves. But I quickly made up for the lack of service with my willingness to please. One-shot drinks were now two shots. Or more. For those who'd seemed to treat me like a fellow human being, I would pour, out of the Scotch or rum bottles, until they said, "Whoa—" Needless to say, the "bar with a Chinese bartender" was popular for a while. When I had to leave, the woman manager almost cried. But the bus had changed routes, and I couldn't find anyone willing to give me rides, not for ten miles each way.

Before that I was a book binder at the Texas Tech University Press. There's not very much to say about a book binder other than you learned to use the glue well. This part of my life experience was omitted in my correspondences to my father.

Before that I worked with my friend Victor (Victor Liu, a heck of a guy) in a Chinese restaurant called Hong Hong. Victor was the Lunch Chef and Second Dinner Chef. I was the Second Lunch Chef and Dinner Dishwasher. The biggest responsibility for me as the Second Lunch Chef was to get the Shanghai Chicken ready to serve. Lubbock people were crazy about Shanghai Chicken at Hong Hong—basically cooked half-chickens dipped in a deep pot of Shanghai Sauce (mostly soy sauce). When a customer ordered it, I was to fish one out from the pot, chop it neatly into eight or ten pieces. Victor, as Lunch Chef, would then add broccoli and a little pepper before sending it out. Chopping the chicken with a meat cleaver was not as easy as it seemed. Victor, the Chef and therefore the master of the kitchen, absolutely forbade chopping the chicken while holding it with another hand. "You might chop off your fingers!" he'd warned. So, done without the use of the other hand, my chopping often sent the pieces flying all over the kitchen. It was like four or five powerful chops with the sharpest cleaver anybody'd ever seen, and I would end up with only two or three pieces in sight. The others I had to pick up from the kitchen floor. Victor didn't care much. He got the pieces from me, wherever they'd been, and served them beautifully with his broccoli.

"Better to serve dirty chicken than your fingers," Victor had said.

Before all that, I lived in my old country.

3. Company Restructuring

How I am hoping that my "end" will come, here at Coldwell, is through an "understanding." It is sort of like I understand I will be fired, and I promise not to make a scene when you fire me. But let's just say that if anybody out there wants to know, you and I will tell him I am not really being fired. Instead, we will tell him, you and I, that there has been a "company restructuring," and as a result, my position has become "untenable," and "with deep regrets" I'll no longer be "with the company."

I don't need to go on and on with this nonsense. The fact is, when all is said and done, you've got to put bread on the table. Period. And you hang on to those little ways you know. You'd better.

Anyway, my biggest complaint now is this dead silence. Around here when it gets quiet, it gets quiet. Even though in Dallas you can't get more "downtown" than where we are—at Main and Pacific, the Coldwell Building. Outside everything is going out of control: people, buses, taxis, delivery vans, the police, the construction crews . . . Outside you can't hear yourself scream. Here in the office it's quiet. Dead quiet. Most of the time, it's like what they say in a commercial about being able to hear a pin drop. And you can *feel* it, too. Every day this great big hush seems to take on more weight. It's really uncomfortable. I mean even physically.

There is simply nothing to do around here. Nothing at all. Since we moved down on the ground floor, away from the rest of the Coldwell business, we, Mary and I, haven't done anything worth mentioning. Not a thing. It's crazy. By the time we finish our morning coffee, we are pretty much done for the day. It would be nice if there were some old files we could sort fifty ways, just to kill time. But they said we should only bring "stationery and personal belongings," and you don't make new files when you do nothing.

I've thought of shutting it all down and going home to play my computer games—no one calls anyway. But I have Mary with me. Mary, my secretary. When they told me to move, Mary moved too—with me, into this terrible quiet. It's kind of funny if you think about it. I mean we used to be a bunch of people. There were people whom I worked for and people who worked for me and all that. We didn't realize it, but we were a real beehive then. Now there's only Mary and me. October 14, 1986. The Day It Really Ended. The day they fired everybody in Coldwell Electronics International, Inc. except the two of us. The Black Friday, if you will. That's almost seven months ago. Then they moved us, in January. After that we waited for the music to end and the lights to go back on, like at the end of the movies. Except we have been waiting and waiting.

I'll tell you about the woman across the hall, just to show you how absolutely "unoccupied" we have been. The woman's small shop is directly across from us. We don't know her at all, never say hello, and she doesn't know us and never says hello and all that. But the woman has a funny way about her. She answers the phone with one hand chopping in the air and waving and pointing as she talks. It looks kind of bad, for a woman. She also sits in a manly way and scowls quite often, at the walls. Anyway, Mary and I joked about her, you know, just for the fun of it. Then we began to think of stories to tell about her life. This became quite a big deal as we got real involved with adding wild details to her life, on daily basis. A total stranger to us, this woman. Mary once had her as a Bulgarian national, then as a spy for the French government, and then there were four very different men who might have fathered her child, a little boy who had "refused to learn to talk." This went on and on for a while. I mean if things went right we could end up spending *hours* making up things. I'd even thought of starting a novel about her.

One day I needed some passport pictures made, so I did the neighborly thing and gave this woman the business—that's what she does, according to her signs, along with TELEXES, FAX, 20-CENT COPIES, and WRAP, PACK AND SHIP. I had just received the government papers for becoming a citizen, so the pictures were a big thing to me. They were to go on my *very first* American passport. Mary thought it was nice too, that I'd go over and "break the ice" and all that. "Tell her I can help with the phone or something, if she has to leave the office sometimes," Mary said.

When I walked into the woman's office, she was quick to smile and greet me. "Yes, sir. What can we do for you?" she said.

"Hi, my name is Eric," I said with much cheerfulness. "I work in the office across the hall . . . " I continued, waiting for her to break into a bigger smile. But she only nodded and seemed a little puzzled.

"Yes?" she said.

"Well . . . I, I just need a couple of pictures made," I said hurriedly.

"Passport or green card?" she asked in a straight voice, business-like, sounding nothing at all like Mary's Bulgarian.

"It's going to be for the passport. I have just passed the examination." I was trying to be casual. "And I'll take the citizen's oath very soon. Possibly next month according to the judge." I raised my voice slightly. You can't help with the rising sense of self-respect when you talk about this kind of thing. "So I thought I'd have my passport pictures made. Now."

"Fourteen dollars," she said.

"Fourteen . . . dollars?"

"Fourteen dollars for two colors. For black-and-white it's nine dollars but you wait twenty minutes. Color ones you don't have to wait. You want color or black-and-white?"

"Color . . . " I said. "I guess."

"Fourteen dollars," she said again.

"Right," I said, and took out my wallet. Afterwards, all that was left were thank-yous and goodbyes. As I turned to leave, I felt, for a moment, that what Mary and I had been saying about her was quite stupid.

We did talk about the woman a couple more times after that day, in our usual crazy ways. Then I simply lost interest. Mary too. There wasn't really anything else we could talk about, still we stopped mentioning the woman altogether.

Anyway, what really gets me most now is to see Mary trying little things to keep us from boring ourselves to death. She'll get a sack of popcorn in some afternoons, or Cokes, or magazines from the tobacco store in the building. She'll read hers and my horo-scope every day from the *Morning News*. This usually lasts a while and gets a laugh or two. Before, there was the gossip she was getting from upstairs, but then my mail was forwarded. Now Mary doesn't go up anymore. Good old Mary. It gets me bad.

Mary was on vacation when they decided to move us down-stairs. This was three months after Black Friday. When she came back, our place was a mess, a real big one. But Mary only started packing and filing things away, packing and filing for days—even came in some nights to clean up. Didn't stop to ask any questions either. Didn't ask then and hasn't asked yet. I have to admit that's really something. Other secretaries would probably go berserk. They would probably insist on knowing what's to become of their "career path" and all that. I mean really.

I'm not saying I don't owe her a good, long explanation. I'm sure I do. And with nothing going on at all, it might not be a bad idea to get into "what's happening" and "what's to happen" a little bit, which, you know, kind of gives you something to hang on to, even if talk like that means very little. For all I know, a nice, long "discussion" may be exactly what we need now. You get paranoid sooner than you think with these long silences going on like mad. But then, I was never told anything about anything either. There was this memo from Carolyn Coldwell to "relocate" me. We moved. And then nothing. Zilch. People don't even call us anymore. I am not saying I can't read the "handwriting on the wall," but whatever they, the "management," have in mind, I sure am not in on it. Granted, they may not have figured out what they are going to say yet, but, still. In other words, the "immedi-ate and long term plans," if any, for the remaining employee(s) at Coldwell Electronics International, Inc., have not been "thoroughly reviewed" with the said employee(s), however faultless he/she/they is/are.

In all fairness, I am not in a hurry to talk to Mary either. First of all, she hasn't asked. Secondly, the entire subject is not what you just "talk about." I mean you can't bring up heavy stuff like this casually, and pretend the worst that can happen is a prolonged five-o'clock traffic. There are "livelihood" and "future" and all that, and you don't *plunge* into any kind of real talk before you are absolutely certain you can at least make it sound semi-decent in the end. And finally, you have to admit there is not a bit of use talking about anything anyway. What's happened has happened. All we can do is wait. I don't mean by waiting a million years things will improve. They may not and may get much worse, but all we can do is wait. This is like being dropped in the center of the ocean. You can kick, you can grab, and you can do a thousand things. All you are doing is wasting yourself away, that's all. No ifs or buts about it, there is nothing we can do. Nothing.

And nothing is exactly what it is. This never-ending nothing.

4. A GLORIOUS MOMENT

I'D SAY SEPTEMBER OF 1972 was when all this started, September 17, 1972, to be exact. My Date of Entry. On that day, as one of a crowd, I got off a Japan Airlines 747 at Los Angeles Airport. I became one of those you'd call "America's new arrivals"—you know, the type of people others like to help a lot. Probably because we were forever grateful for anybody who had time to tell us a thing or two. For the officers at the Immigration, I was a "Non-Resident Alien." From them I received a card that I had to fill out every year on New Year's Day and a sheet that said if I ever looked for a job I'd be "subject to deportation."

It was about five or six in the afternoon when I got off. I saw the orange sun through the airplane windows. I saw lots of people in the airport. And, right there and then, I became so excited I almost went berserk. It must have been quite a sight, if anybody noticed, the way I looked as I came off the plane. If you hang around these huge airports at all, you probably see it a thousand times a day: big planes dumping off big bunches of people. Most of them look like they are about to throw up or whatever; then there are likely to be the two or three small, scrawny guys, four at most, hit as hard as I was back then, by whatever it was that hit me, wandering about with such wild eyes you think the best possible thing for them is a dunk in a clear pool. I was excited. You could've offered a trip to the moon and couldn't have gotten me more interested. The arrival—a glorious moment. There were people passing me in all directions, and I stood, confused, tired, ecstatic, and for no good reasons, proud.

It was quite something I did, now that I look back, to have come a million miles, by myself, and actually *arrived* here. Granted, many others had done it before, but, still. Besides, there was not a lot to hang on to, at the time. I mean there was not even a number that I had to call "immediately after arrival." No one in any way connected to me, my family, or my ancestors since Day One had set foot on this land. In fact, there was no possibility of running into someone I "might know." And I had no money either. Well, four hundred dollars. That was about the last of my father's savings. I must admit I wiped my old man out by coming here.

I don't believe I qualified as one of those you saw on TV who "immigrated for greater opportunities" or "sought refuge from political persecutions." Nothing *forced* me or anything. Sure, we didn't have a lot of what you'd call "freedom" back home, what with the police inviting themselves into your home whenever they liked and all that—and you'd be gracious as hell if no one was taken away. But that didn't bother me much—we didn't know enough to tell the difference anyway. As for money, it was quite a different story. It was kind of rough from time to time. Then again, I was not dumb enough to think coming here was any great solution, like someone in good old Los Angeles was going to give me a sack of fifty-dollar bills to "enjoy at my own discretion" or something.

What happened was there had been a feeling, you might call it "urge," that I had experienced for the longest time that made me come here. It's hard to explain, but it felt like either America or the end of the world. Pretty strong stuff. And I was not the only one—a bunch of us had been affected. My classmates, relatives, friends, enemies—even teachers at the University who had called it unpatriotic to "abandon the motherland," now that the "Red Bandits" had reduced it to a mere island. A bunch of us. And one by one, one way or the other, some of us did come here. I did in '72. Those who didn't must have had it hard. From what I've heard they are doing just great now, making all sorts of money and all that, but you've got to feel sorry for how they felt at the time.

Anyway, I was all cooped up in this tiny corner of the world, then came this feeling, or "urge," then came this letter that called me "Mr. Chung" and told me how happy they were to give me "a place in the graduate program," and how confident they were about my "eventually making contributions to the curriculum at Texas Tech." That was enough reason for me.

So here I was, all worked up and delirious at the Los Angeles Airport, when this man in uniform came my way.

"Over there," he said.

"Huh?" I said. His badge was shining silver. There was no possibility for me to figure out what he wanted from me.

"Over there," he said again. And I still didn't understand. The truth was, I couldn't make out the words he was speaking. You'd think any second-rate country with a second-rate civilization would teach their citizens some decent English, so that by the time they are high-school graduates, they would at least know the words "over" and "there." Well, mine did, and, believe me, I knew both words, by heart. But this man was speaking them faster than any of my lousy teachers could in a million years. And for the life of me, I could not figure out the words.

"I beg your pardon?" I said very slowly. I knew this sentence would buy me some time in any situation. I had to get myself oriented and gathered quickly, in order to respond to this man with any intelligence.

By this time the man must have concluded that there was some kind of problem with me. He took one more step forward, looked me straight in the eyes, his voice full of calmness and patience, and said the equivalent of: "This is not where you belong, your line is over there." I have no way of knowing if that was in fact what he said. At the time it was only a string of blurry sounds much longer than the one made by "over there." It's not hard now to figure out what had happened. I went to a short and fast-moving line as I was trying to go through the Customs. What I should've done was to go with the much longer line that didn't seem to be moving at all. The short lines were for U. S. citizens only. And the man in uniform was good enough to spot a "Non-Resident Alien" one mile away. "I beg your pardon?" I said again. I was then in a genuine panic. I tried like hell to get any meaning out of anything. I would've begged this man to take all my money if that would've done any good.

The man tried again. And, bless his heart, again and again. He got more serious each time he started over. Poor man. He knew he had a bad case on his hands and was probably beginning to realize how unbecoming it was of him to pick on me. We must have gone back and forth like this:

"I beg your pardon?"

(Hesitation.) "This line is for American citizens only, sir. Are you an American citizen? If you're not, you have to go to that line over there, please." (Pointing and gesturing.)

(Pause. Face turned whiter.) "I . . . I beg your pardon?" (Voice almost gone. Eyes begging for forgiveness.)

"Just go to that line, sir. That way. Over there!" (Forced smile. Faster gestures.) "You're all right there!"

"Huh?" (Head lowered.)

"Okay. You see these lines? Line one, two, and three. Those are not for you. No. Don't go there." (Pointing and waving.) "Those lines over there . . . " (More pointing and waving.) "Those officers will help you. Officers . . . " (Pointing at himself.) "Will help you!" (Pointing at me.) "Okay? Go over there. Any lines over there."

(Something began to make sense.) (Tiny voice inside said, "Could he, by any chance, be asking me to go to that mile-long line that's hardly moving . . . ?") "Over there?" (Everything bet on this last try.) (Most important now for a positive response from this man.) (Anything in the vein of "Attaboy!" or "By George, I think he's got it!" would do.)

"Well . . . " (Shook head.) "I tell you what." (Up in arms.) "You stay here, don't move. Stay. We'll find help. Help." (Pointed to a room.) "Don't move. Understand?" (Ignored my second attempt to say "Over there?") (Left.)

Anyway, he was gone for about twenty minutes. I was devastated. I didn't even take a step away from the exact spot I was standing. There was cold sweat all over me. It was like I was in the middle of a gigantic misunderstanding. I am not saying I was any good with English, that wasn't the case at all. But there had never been any problem passing the tests. Somehow I felt that my university had agreed that I'd been at least "adequate." We'd even studied Shakespeare. And the man was obviously not doing anything close to Shakespeare. I felt like a creep who'd lost everything he'd owned. It was terrible. I must have looked bad then, real bad.

The man finally came back with an interpreter and you can pretty much guess the rest. I was out of the Customs in ten minutes. I was so exhausted I didn't even thank the interpreter. There was no way I could think straight anymore.

On the same day, I was to make a connection to Albuquerque, New Mexico, stay there for one and a half hours, then catch another flight to Lubbock, Texas. I knew nothing about Albuquerque, and was happy to leave it at that. Lubbock was to be my final destination. The document I was holding, U. S. Government Form I-20, basically told me I must report to Texas Tech in Lubbock or else.

Before coming here, I had checked with several books in the library about Lubbock, knowing it was going to be my new home and all that. In a book about American geography there was a paragraph or two on Lubbock. They talked about the weather, deserts, and cowboys and Indians. I quickly discounted all that, being a man of common sense. Then the librarian showed me a florists' trade magazine with a list of American cities, indicating Lubbock had twenty-three flower shops. This made my father quite happy. Our city had only about five, and we were a big city by any standard.

"A city with twenty-three flower shops must be very prosperous," my father said. That was enough to get him, and me, gladly back on our normal lives.

I was mostly quiet on the flights from Los Angeles to Albuquerque to Lubbock. There was no point in starting a conversation with anybody. It would've been suicide. Besides, I needed to sort out the situation I'd gotten myself in. First of all, I was now in America. It was now fact. I couldn't turn back because there was no money. Second of all, the English skills were now suddenly as important as life and death, and mine had been downgraded from "adequate" to "severely handicapped." And lastly, I desperately needed to know if there was any possible way I could go to the graduate school without looking like a total imbecile. Things were getting out of hand. There was a lot of doom and gloom in my thoughts, I must admit. Like I was playing in a big game and forgot all the rules. It was suddenly important to watch others carefully. You could always copy someone. That way you'd never end up being the only fool.

When I landed in Lubbock, several people were already waiting. The school had been kind, and smart enough to arrange for students from my country to meet me. I was obviously not the first trauma case. Wasn't going to be last either. They wanted to make sure I came in all right and that, in about a week, I'd be able to walk on my own two feet into the Admissions Office. There were stories of new foreign students who'd taken the next flights home. And of a girl from my country who, within days of her arrival, became a member of the "Chinese mafia." Of course these might be only stories. But the Chinese students at Texas Tech loved to talk about them.

The leader of this welcoming committee was a guy who owned a car and had driven the party there. It was Victor Liu. He was the first person I met in Lubbock. I noticed his dark, thick eyebrows and piercing eyes right away. There was him, another guy, and two girls. They all looked at me for the longest time. The other guy offered to help with the luggage. The girls spoke softly to each other and giggled occasionally. They both wore mini-dresses.

As we got in the car, I was immediately impressed with the air conditioning. Back home I only rode in taxis and buses, and they never had air conditioning. Fuel was too expensive for any kind of comfort. The girls, one of them humming an American song, were quite pleased too. Victor cheerfully drove away. He shifted the gears and pushed a button to clean the windshield. The water shot out from the bottom of the windshield while the wipers wiped. I was truly amazed, not having seen similar performances before.

"How . . . how come the water comes up from the bottom?" I said, inspired, showing signs of life to my countrymen for the first time.

"Oh, yeah . . . " Victor was delighted. He shifted his gears again. "Everything in this country is upside down," he said, as he sped up. "Everything." He nodded, then he looked at me with a touch of sympathy, and said, "You just watch."

5. FULLY UTILIZED

IF THERE WAS ONE PERSON who changed my life in America—
I am skipping way ahead in my story—it was Roger Holton.
Roger Holton got me in Mr. Coldwell's business. *The* Mr. *Malcolm* Coldwell. Chances are you already know how big Mr. Coldwell is, and you know, too, how much it means to be *in* Mr.
Coldwell's business. It's not like I was just an employee. It's much more.

First, Roger introduced himself to Mr. Coldwell at a party.
Then he got Mr. Coldwell interested in a business idea. Then he talked Mr. Coldwell into investing in this idea. Then he had both him and me hired in this business, with me working under him.
And, on top of all that, Mr. Coldwell agreed that as soon as the business began to make money, Roger and I would be made partners of the business, Roger a bigger partner than I. Roger pulled the whole thing off. One miracle after another. Your average man on the street couldn't even get second glances from Mr.
Coldwell's secretaries. The world was full of people who "only needed five minutes" of Mr. Coldwell's "valuable time." I don't know how exactly Roger did it. That Roger, he was something else.

· · ·

Roger first told me about Mr. Coldwell in the spring of 1979 when we were at the Jojo's on Spring Valley. For me the place was only five minutes' walk from where I was working at the time, Taltex's main building in north Dallas. Roger worked downtown; he had to drive thirty minutes on that day "in the worst traffic," he said, just so that we could "meet and lunch." I was then in my seventh year in the States, things were generally slow for me, and a little boring. But I had a quiet feeling that, somehow, my life was *improving*, that I'd seen my worst days in America.

I'd recently been promoted to Systems Programmer/Analyst Two at Taltex. My boss, the Systems Programming Manager, was beginning to realize, after two and a half years, that I might have "long-term potentials" because everybody else in my department either had quit or was quitting. So now I was kind of looking forward to becoming a Senior Systems Programmer/Analyst in twelve months (as a "fast-track rising star") or, at most, in three years (if I didn't make a lot of mistakes). Things were not bad for me at the time; I was taking more long lunches than ever. I was also using bigger words in my memos. Like "accordingly," "corresponding to," "retrospective," and so on.

Roger was with Taltex too, in the Corporate Marketing Group. His title was Market Communications Manager. Basically, what he did was to set up Taltex booths and displays at the large electronics conventions you sometimes read about in the newspapers. Taltex always sent an army of salesmen to these conventions. They used the booths and displays to give customers the sales talk. Roger had three people working for him, and he traveled a lot to be wherever the conventions were. He had hired Darth Vader once to sign posters by the booth. Since then he'd carried a picture of him and Darth Vader together, before a bright Taltex sign. Roger's job grade at Taltex was 28, mine was 26. Roger had been with Taltex for seventeen years when we had our talk at Jojo's.

"Eric, I'm leaving Taltex," Roger said, as soon as we sat down at a table by the window. From where we were, we could see the top part of the glass Taltex buildings shining under the sun. Roger was in a suit, which was unusual for a Taltex employee of his job grade. Only Department Managers (job grade: 36 or 38), Division Vice Presidents (job grade: 40), and the President (no job grade) wore suits at Taltex. Branch Managers (job grade: 34) put on ties now and then but never coats or suits. People ranking lower, Roger and I included, should be in "casual, but decent" clothes of some kind (meaning shirt-and-pants for most of us). The company originally banned formal clothes altogether to "encourage a hard-working and friendly culture." Sometime back the rule bent, but only for the top guys because of their "customer-related functions." Roger, however, was always formal with a dark suit, white shirt, and expensive silk tie. Add to that his short hair, his clean-shaven red face, his six-foot-two height, and his broad shoulders, he looked, to me, as important as any executive.

"I gave Ron and Henry my resignation this morning," Roger continued. Ron was Roger's boss; and Henry, a Branch Manager, was Ron's boss. I never did learn Ron's last name. Or Henry's. Another big thing at Taltex, other than what to wear, was that all employees were to be addressed by their first names only. To this there were no exceptions, not even the President, Fred.

"Why?" I gave him a raised voice out of politeness. I was more interested in why he wanted to talk to me. You couldn't possibly be surprised about anybody's quitting. There were over seventy thousand employees at Taltex, and at least half of them talked about quitting on a daily basis. Not that there was anything seriously wrong with the company. Considering only a handful would eventually make it to the top, a great majority of the seventy thousand were bound to feel, one way or the other, not "fully utilized." Roger, after seventeen years, was unlikely an exception.

Roger had asked me to do some translation work for him once. That had been my only dealing with him. He was expecting a delegation from China to come through his booths at the Consumer Electronics Show in Las Vegas, and he wanted some brochures in Chinese. He had paid me well for the job. And I wanted to know, quitting or no quitting, if he was going to ask me again.

"Well," Roger said, mysteriously, "I have been offered a very good opportunity."

"Oh, that's great!" I said, again out of politeness. People always told you they quit Taltex to work for a company "that really cared about its people" and all that.

"Yeah, and that's why I want to talk to you."

"Yeah?"

"Yeah. You know those brochures you helped me translate for the Las Vegas show?"

"Yes?"

"You did great. That was a wonderful job you did. People liked it a lot."

"You mean the Chinese?"

"Yes, we've had very good comments about them. And that's what I want to talk to you about."

"You mean you want to make more Chinese brochures?" I said with delight.

"No . . . Well, what I am about to do is much more." Roger looked me straight in the eyes. He moved his elbows forward on the table. Bright light from outside picked up the calm, elegant colors of his suit. I could see he had great confidence, that he was about to impress the hell out of me. "I might as well tell you. But please, please, this is only between you and me."

"Sure, Roger, sure."

"Well, Eric, I have been asked to develop business in China for the wealthiest man in the United States."

"You, you mean . . . Rockefeller?"

"No, Eric. But this man is just as wealthy. And he knows the Rockefellers too. His name is Malcolm Coldwell. Mr. Coldwell."

"Who is he?" I said quickly. I felt the conversation was becoming more than I could handle.

"He is . . . I'm sure you've heard of him." Roger sounded disappointed. He turned toward the window. "You see these buildings around us? Mr. Coldwell owns most of them. If you ask around, you'll know."

"Oh." I saw outside a couple of children playing on the sidewalk. The top parts of the Taltex buildings were too bright to look at.

"Anyway, he's one of the most influential men in the United States. Certainly the most influential in Texas. He wants to develop a relationship with China. He believes in it. A big business. We're talking big investment." Roger looked satisfied. He leaned back and crossed his arms. "It's like Armand Hammer. Have you heard of Armand Hammer?"

"No . . . " My voice lowered.

"Armand Hammer developed a relationship with the Russian government from way back. He was the one who got the Russians to give him an exclusive franchise for selling arms to them. Now he is probably the richest man in the world."

"You mean . . . richer than Malc . . . Malc . . . richer than the guy you told me about?"

"I wouldn't say so, but they are all very important, you know." Roger was becoming impatient. "You know these are people who really run this country. You don't see them in the newspapers every day. But they are the ones that really count."

"Oh."

"And Mr. Coldwell, who's widowed and childless, is well known for surrounding himself with sharp young men and giving them the complete authority to run his business."

"Oh."

"Getting back to the point, Mr. Coldwell wants me to see what he can do with China. He commissioned me to do some work. I've been to China twice already to talk to the government." Roger slowly stirred his coffee.

"Yeah?" Roger must have seen how I suddenly brightened up. I was beginning to feel a pure sense of respect for the man. It was 1979. Nobody went to China in the 1970s. Nobody but Nixon and Kissinger. There I was, a Chinese by birth and education, fluent only in Chinese, but knowing as much about China as any good old boy from Seminole, Texas, population 236. I must admit I was *awed*. This man, Roger Holton, Market Communication Manager, job grade 28, could easily become my hero. He only had to convince me what he had said was true. And the way things were going, it was not going to be hard either. It was now important to find out as much as I could. "Well," I muttered, "what do you want me to do?"

"I need your help," Roger replied. He was very much at ease with himself. "I can't do all this by myself. I need all kinds of people to help me. We are building a big business, from the ground up. We must draw the best talents into this." Roger spoke evenly and thoughtfully; he squinted at the Taltex buildings. Outside the lunch traffic was thinning out, now even the streets were shiny under the sun. "That is," he turned to me, "if you are interested. You have the language and cultural skills. You have a good head. From what I can see, you are a quick-study also. This is going to be a tough business—no one has done what we are about to do. And we, Mr. Coldwell and I, need people who can really contribute. People like you."

"Well . . . Thank you, Roger . . . "

The rest of the conversation was fairly straightforward. Every word Roger had to say was music to my ears. I remember mumbling a lot, about what a "tremendous career challenge" it was to be in the China business with him, and how I saw myself devoting the "rest of my life" to it. Basically, what came out in the end was that I agreed to help him put a plan together, without pay. He'd then present the plan to Mr. Coldwell. There was to be a meeting two months later of Mr. Coldwell, his top advisers, and Roger. Once the plan was approved, I was to quit Taltex and join him as "one of the first employees" of this business. And that would be the beginning of our being able to "forget all our worries."

When I returned to work, a good one and a half hours after the lunch break, the computer terminal, the desk, the thick technical books and everything within fifty yards of my seat looked just about the most miserable things I had ever seen. My life as a Programmer/Analyst Two, job grade 26, had turned most seriously dull. I felt very happy about the future, and very lucky. I felt bad for my fellow Systems Programmer/Analysts, all of them six to eight job grades away from wearing a tie, and a good twelve to fourteen job grades away, if they could ever make it, from a suit. I also felt a sense of warmth, for the first time in two and a half years, for my boss, the Systems Programming Manager.

In the next few years I was able to gather, piece by piece, the general truth about how Roger had gotten started with Mr. Coldwell and with the China business. Roger had never been to China like he told me at Jojo's. He never went to China, period, until much later, when he went with me. He had all the Chinese brochures in Las Vegas, and nobody ever showed up to look at them, except a man who called himself Professor Zhang. Roger ended up spending a long time talking to this Professor Zhang, you know, just to shoot the breeze. Professor Zhang later wrote Roger a letter from China, telling Roger that he was "welcomed to come to China" some day. And that was it, in total, the entire "China connection" for Roger—Professor Zhang, a nice chat, and one letter.

A few months after the Las Vegas show, Roger was at a fund-raising party as a volunteer worker representing Taltex. He was walking through the crowd, delivering a drink to his boss Ron's wife, when he overheard a man talking about China. The man, sixtyish, white-haired, and raspy-voiced, did not have much to say about China other than his niece had been trying to get invited to the Canton Fair. He had the undivided attention, though, from the expensively-dressed younger men and women around him. Roger stopped to listen, and before you knew it, he made himself heard.

"Excuse the interruption, sir, but I had some dealings with China," Roger said. He went directly up to the man and volunteered more: "And the key to dealing with the Chinese is to have proper introductions. It's very important, *most* important—having proper introductions." Good old Roger. He stopped briefly, allowing the man a good look at him, and continued with a raised voice to address the whole group. "Speaking from experience, I do believe a good relationship, or connection, with certain high ranking Communist party officials can open doors, many kinds of doors."

The man was apparently intrigued by Roger. None of his followers, the good-looking men and women, turned away. So Roger proceeded to tell all he knew about China, which was very little. But everyone listened—for about twenty minutes. Roger didn't forget to mention Professor Zhang. He called Professor's letter "an official invitation to visit China for business discussions." And that it was "extremely rare," this invitation, because nobody else had ever gotten one. "I've worked hard at getting my invitation," Roger said to the man before leaving the group, "for a long, long time."

The man turned out to be Mr. Coldwell, the sponsor of the party.

Anyway, Mr. Coldwell and Roger exchanged business cards. When Roger tried later to find out about Mr. Coldwell, he must have gotten the same treatment as he was to give me, from whomever he asked.

But Roger saw a possibility. He saw an opening in his life. And he went for it, with everything he had. He called up Mr. Coldwell a few days later and said the Chinese had contacted him again, "through official channels," and that he felt Mr. Coldwell might be interested in the "content of this communication." When everything was said and done, before Roger came to talk to me at Jojo's, there had only been a couple of meetings between him and Mr. Coldwell. In the second meeting, there were also Mr. Coldwell's lawyers and consultants. And, this time, did Roger put on a show. I mean really. Roger himself described it to me later in glorious details. Everybody saw the *scenario*. Roger's *scenario*. Nothing but Roger's *scenario*. It went like this:

The Chinese trusted Roger. The Chinese did not trust too many Americans because the United States had been hostile for over thirty years. The Chinese government now wanted to do business. Big business. They wanted to "modernize." They wanted relationships with important American businessmen, and they didn't know how to go about it. But they trusted Roger. And they also knew he, as a "senior executive" in an American corporation, had contacts with important American businessmen. Through him they wanted to do business with important American businessmen. Enter Mr. Coldwell, the important American businessman.

Anyway, at the end of the second meeting a deal was struck. Roger was to find out exactly what the Chinese wanted, then put "the numbers" together for Mr. Coldwell. They agreed to meet again in two months. In the meantime, Mr. Coldwell gave Roger a check, 1500 dollars, for "interim expenses." Fifteen hundred lousy dollars. And Roger was on the way to the biggest game in his life. He was ready to quit Taltex right there and then. You couldn't help but respect him. He had the right stuff. He wanted to begin living *his* life, bad.

I also found out later that one of Mr. Coldwell's men had been smart enough to ask, in the second meeting, how Roger planned to overcome his "unfamiliarity" with the Chinese language, culture, and all that. Roger first responded bravely that he'd studied Chinese at Yale. Then he admitted the need for a "native Chinese speaker." He told Mr. Coldwell the Chinese contingency in Washington, D.C., was so interested in the project they had recommended an "overseas Chinese" to him.

That's how I came into the picture.

I remember well what Roger said as we walked out of Jojo's. "Eric," he said, " I want you to be there in the next meeting with the Coldwell people. This time you and I are going to blow them away with our operational plans. We are going to get the whole business going, right there and then. We are going to ask for about thirty million." I remember how he opened his car door and then raised his head to look at a flock of high-flying birds. I remember how he shook my hand and patted my shoulder as we were parting. There was no room for any doubt from me. Or from himself. He, Roger Holton, was in command. Nothing could possibly stand in his way. He'd let you know it, too. By the way he spoke his words, the way he inspected the things around us as we walked. A totally realized master of the situations—his, and possibly mine. The great Roger Holton himself. The one and only. You couldn't *deny* him.

6. THE WAY YOU SAY DALLAS

ROGER CHANGED MY LIFE HERE, but it was Victor Liu who first taught me how to *see* America. Around him Victor was able to see strength, plentifulness, and opportunities. He also saw himself right in the middle of it all—a picture of himself in an exciting new world. A picture he readily shared with me and other new students in Lubbock. It might have been what we needed too; all of us were having it tough with our shares of "hard reality." Years later, Victor's picture would turn bleak, but at the time, it was somewhat of a hope and a way through desperation for us—and a wonderful setting for his own courageous drive.

"Lubbock has tall buildings," I wrote to my family in 1972, three days after I had arrived in this country. "But the land is quite big and flat, so all buildings, tall or short, look small. I do have some problems with the way people speak their English. This difficulty will, most probably, disappear in the next week or two. People here seem quite friendly, though. Will try to send photos soon."

I was living in Sneed Hall, a university dormitory. My roommate for three weeks was a young man who had, only three months before, graduated from high school. We talked very little. I spent most of my time, including weekends, in the library trying to figure out what had gone on in my classes at the graduate school. I remember giving the guy a pair of embroidered slippers (made in my country) when he told me one night that it was his birthday. I remember him telling me he was a little scared because he didn't know if he was going to make it. I couldn't quite understand what he meant, so we didn't get into that. A few days later his father came and took him away. By then, I was beginning to meet more and more students from my country. I saw them very often at the library and the school post office. The girls always cried when they got letters from home.

Victor quickly became popular among the new arrivals. The other second- or third-year students from my country who had cars stayed away from us. (That meant we walked a lot. The sixteen blocks to the bank was not too bad, and the supermarket was only four blocks to the east of the campus, with the sidewalks nicely shaded by the buildings.) But Victor usually was agreeable when we asked for rides—that is, if we had a small group going to the same places and if we'd give him at least one day's notice. He didn't get impatient with us. The others did because we asked the dumbest questions all the time. But we couldn't keep quiet because we *had* to know. With Victor we did not have to ask much. He voluntarily gave us information which he *knew* we needed. Even with his busy work on the Ph. D. and as a teaching assistant at the physics department, Victor seemed to enjoy taking us around, telling us things.

"You see the sign on my right?" Victor stopped his car and turned to talk; we were leaving the campus on one of our trips to the bank. "That's called a 'stop sign', and you have to stop, like the sign says." Victor pointed. "It's not like back home where you don't stop unless you have to. Here you have to. Or the police will get you."

We all paid good attention to Victor. It was only the second week of school. Most of us had not been off campus much. Victor's rides were a good way to visit our new city. After a turn on the University Avenue, Victor continued, "It's important to stay in your lane, after you make the turns, like what I just did. America is strict on this, too. And you have to use your blinkers when you make a turn." Victor stopped at a red light. "I'm telling you this because you're all going to drive sooner or later, and you need to know."

"Can you drive all the way to Dallas? Is there a road?" asked George. George was in Food and Nutrition. He had on a pair of heavy glasses and was wearing a white shirt. The others in the car were Edward, Electrical Engineering, Frank, Economics, Tang-I, Mechanical Engineering, and me, Computer Sciences. Tang-I didn't have an English name at the time; he had said he'd use Tom, but still wanted to talk to the Foreign Student Advisor.

"Of course you can drive there. Nonstop," Victor said. "There are highways to everywhere. That's why it's important to have a car. You should get a map. You really should." Then he turned and looked at George. "You must change the way you say that city."

"Oh?" George became a little uneasy. So did the rest of us. We couldn't tell what was wrong with the way he'd said Dallas.

"You should say it like I do." Victor was kind enough to enunciate the city's name two more times, but we still couldn't tell the difference.

"I can't tell the difference, please—"

"Of course you can't," Victor interrupted Tang-I. "Your ears are not used to the sounds of American English yet. You've got to learn American English. If you talk with an accent, you'll not be accepted. It's very important. When you've lived here longer —I've been here for two and half years—you'll hear the differences. 'DAH-LAS,' that's the way you say it. 'DEL-LAS,' that's the way I say it. Dellas. Dellas. Dellas."

"Dallas. Dallas. Dallas . . . " George began practicing aloud. Victor patiently helped him every time. Then the rest of us, too. We were each corrected at least fifteen times. By the time we made the turn into the bank's parking lot, we could pretty well pronounce Dallas right. Somewhat like "Dellas."

"That's more like it." Victor sighed. He turned off the engine.

"Thank you, Victor," we all said.

"You're welcome. Oh—" Victor opened the car door and quickly pulled it back. He turned to make sure we were all still in the car. "I'll see you get a real orientation in a few days. A special *new student* orientation. I think you'll learn a lot." Victor grinned, then he looked down at his watch to think. We all waited in silence.

"Just make sure I can find you in the library either this Friday night or the next. Around nine o'clock." Victor concluded his announcement with a quick glance at us. We were all very curious, but none of us asked for more details. We knew that this wonderful orientation, or whatever, was definitely going to happen now that Victor had promised. There was no reason to get *anxious* or anything. Victor opened the car door and stepped out.

"Okay . . . " we all said, following Victor out of the car and into the bank.

·   ·   ·

In less than a year, Victor was to drop his Ph. D. study to work for a big company. Before he left in the summer of 1973, we—I, George, Frank, Tang-I, and a couple of the new students—had lived either in dorms or very close by, and Victor had, in many ways, been the center of our lives. We didn't think of him as indispensable or anything, but he was the man to ask for help, any help. He showed us how you could file a penny down to the size of a dime to buy Cokes. And how we could reuse the stamps not marked by the post office. There was a kind of attitude about him that we liked a lot. He was as clumsy in America as any of us. We all knew it, too. But he kept coming up with his own smart ways, just to show he'd managed, and once in a while, something actually worked for him. None of us knew if we were going to get anywhere at all in this new country. Victor included. The rest of us were mostly too afraid to give anything a try, to *step out*. Not Victor. He was not afraid.

One day George's classmate was giving George and me a hard time. His classmate had returned from the Vietnam War and the Far East, and had a few bad things to say about Oriental culture in general. He thought our country was dirty, backward, and our government was corrupt. It was really not far from the truth, but George was not about to let him get away with it. The thing was, all George could manage to say were many "But . . . "s and "No . . . "s. His classmate, a Mass Communications minor, showed no signs of accommodation.

"There's no doubt about it, fundamental changes must take place or your government will only hurt your country more," the classmate insisted, halfway into the conversation.

"No . . . that's not right . . . " George's face was red. We were sitting in the lobby of the library. George's raised voice was beginning to bother others.

"Face it: backward political system, next to nothing in natural resources—what future do you have if you don't start organizing for economic activities?"

"But . . . no . . . I think—"

"Look at Europe, for instance: the organization comes naturally, because the people are naturally organized. The culture naturally organizes them. A society of order. You don't have any order, you don't know what order is. Just look at the traffic, the pickpockets, and the beggars—"

"No, you're wrong—"

"No, *you* are wrong. I know what I saw. Neither your government nor anybody can fool me."

George was about to explode. He kept pushing up his thick glasses. His hands trembled. I felt terrible, too. Not because of what was said. I wanted George, as one of us, to be able to stand up whenever he wished. I wanted to see him *handle* the situation. But George didn't even know where to begin. Neither did I. We sat there and saw this guy score more and more points on us. There didn't seem to be an end in sight. He was totally dominating the conversation.

Suddenly, Victor came from nowhere and plumped down on the sofa next to George. He was smart enough to know, immediately, what was going on.

"Your culture wanes!" Victor said with fire. His voice echoed in the big library lobby.

"What?" The classmate didn't know what to make of it. His eyes opened wide. George and I looked at each other with joy. Victor had always said you had to "get back at Americans" with

"sharp words" and "attack them as hard as they attack you."
We knew Victor was saying something like the American culture
was going down the drain. It didn't matter what Victor said. He
talked back.

"I abominate your culture!" Victor declared. He didn't give
the classmate any time to think on the part about the waning
culture.

"Huh?" The classmate was totally confused.

"Yeah, I abominate your culture!" George almost yelled. He,
too, saw the chance for a small triumph.

"Yeah! I abominate too!" I said.

"Yeah! I abominate too!" It was Sherri Chang, Home Economics, from behind me. We didn't know when she'd invited
herself in.

The classmate was amazed. He had no idea the debate was
turning into a real battle. And with so many people "abominat-
ing" whatever it was, he saw no way of coming out in any decent
shape. He picked up his books and left.

We sat up all night to talk about it. Everyone was elated. Most
of all, Victor and George. The girls left us when the library
closed. We moved to George's room in the dorm and began to
sing. First we sang any songs that came to our minds. Then we
settled on the three songs that all of us knew: "Killing Me Softly
With His Song," "Edelweiss," and "I Could Have Danced All
Night." We sang louder and louder. When someone banged on
the wall, we moved to the lawn in front of the dorm. We sang the
three songs over and over again. It was very dark outside, and we
could not see each other's faces. By the way the voices were
broken, we knew some of us were crying. And when Victor quickly
wiped his face with the back of his hand, we were surprised that

he, too, had cried. But we kept singing, same three songs, over and over again. In fact, we were shouting into the darkness. With all our strength we shouted and shouted. Every word of the three songs, again and again. Waiting for the first light of the morning to make us stop.

7. Preliminary Proposals

WITHIN THREE TO FOUR WEEKS of our meeting at Jojo's, Roger and I had worked on at least a dozen "preliminary proposals" to present to Mr. Coldwell:

The Development of Comprehensive Import-Export Industrial and Special Economic Trade Zone in the Greater Shanghai Metropolitan Area—A Preliminary Proposal

A Preliminary Proposal for the Coal Gasification and Liquefaction Process in Shanxi Province and Subsequent Developments

Basic Concept and Preliminary Proposal for a Rapid Buildup of a Network of Hotels and Passenger Transportation Services (Air Included) in China

Revamping of Semiconductor Manufacturing—The Most Needed Step in Chinese Modernization (Preliminary Proposal)

Inland and Offshore Oil Drilling in Partnership with the Chinese Government—A First Look and Preliminary Proposal

A Preliminary Proposal for Retrofitting Chinese Machine Tools for Numeric Control Purposes — Nationwide Applications

A Preliminary Proposal for Data Base Management for Chinese National Banking Systems

Etc.

Etc.

There were a few about arms sales too (what was good for Armand Hammer was good for Mr. Coldwell). Also one about the fast-food chains and another about starting up professional sports. I have to say Roger and I worked pretty hard in those days. Mr. Coldwell's business was mainly insurance; he himself had started as an insurance salesman. We had no thoughts of branching Coldwell Life into China, though. The Chinese government, for a ton of reasons, was not about to let in any foreigners to sell life insurance. Period. Although with things like "cultural revolution" cropping up once in a while, those millions who'd died could have made some use of it. Since Mr. Coldwell was a man of "tremendous wealth," Roger said, he could pretty much do whatever he wanted. Millions of possibilities. Insurance was only one.

The thing was, Roger kept coming up with different plans. "Think of Mr. Coldwell and China combining their resources," Roger said. "Just think of it. Doesn't it boggle your mind what enormous, extraordinary things they could do together? That's why it's so important, Eric, that we, as engineers of the projects, come up with the right plans."

So, night after night, we worked on different ideas.

•   •   •

Granted, we knew little of what we were doing. Looking back, I have to admit we were very much out of our minds for coming up with one scheme after another about "modernizing" China—with other people's money, too. But, still.

"It's like this," I reported my new enterprise to my father in a letter. "A billion people in that big country, and all they let you know up till now is they loved red flags. Now things have changed, and they say to you, 'Okay, we are tired of shouting political slogans all day long. We want some of the fun you've been having, and we like the smell of money, too. Let's talk business.'"

My father had not long before sold his business and put most of the proceeds into a small piece of land. "Keep up the good work," he wrote back. He'd said the same when I told him I had become a computer programmer. I could pretty much write him whatever I wanted, which he'd enjoy tremendously, as long as there was no request of money.

"It's impossible for one to understand China today," I continued in the letter. "No one does. Not the billion people themselves. Not the old, bullheaded bureaucrats who are supposedly in charge—they are only interested in keeping each other from gaining more power. And certainly not Roger or I or anybody we know, for that matter. The truth is, we are groping in the dark."

For this part of the letter my father had no response.

Roger and I had a heck of time trying to go more than four or five pages on any of the stuff we were working on. Pretty soon the proposals all read like garbage. And we were soon running out of time. Roger wrote at least five or six letters to Professor Zhang, and heard nothing back. Then he insisted the two of us go to Washington to "clear things up" directly with the Chinese ambassador. But the airfare was out of reach for Roger's fifteen-hundred-dollar budget, so we ended up visiting the Chinese consulate in Houston. The trip to Houston didn't turn out to be much of a help.

We thought the people at the consulate would be more than happy to receive us as "representatives of Mr. Coldwell." They probably were, only the guy they chose to see us was unreal. He definitely had my vote for the one most likely to succeed in world-class poker tournaments. I mean you couldn't get him to move his eyebrow one thousandth of an inch, let alone his lips. Roger did all the talking, for about one hour. The man did nothing but take notes. He wrote furiously. But he kept his face strictly the same. It was quite a sight. Roger went on with all his big talk about Mr. Coldwell, and suggested that the Consulate should help find ways of "mutual cooperations" and all that. When Roger finished, there was nothing but a long silence. The official only stopped writing, his face did not change. Even Roger was getting funny feelings. He turned to me and asked that I say the same thing all over in Chinese. That didn't make a lot of sense, because the man had obviously understood. But I went on anyway, in Chinese. Sure enough, the man started taking notes again. Furiously. By the time I finished, it had been a good one and a half hours. There was again the silence. Roger and I had only the ceiling and the floor to stare at. Finally, the man spoke.

"Thank you for your talk. We will consider."

"Great." Roger smiled with relief. "Please let us hear from you as soon as you have an idea. And please bear in mind that Mr. Coldwell is very important politically and in business. China should consider a major project that might best take advantage of his capabilities."

"We will consider," the man said. As he stood up to shake our hands goodbye, I noticed his Mao suit was quite wrinkled. Roger then showed the man his letter from Professor Zhang. The man only took more notes.

Roger believed those notes would be published and read "throughout the party," and we'd hear something back soon, "directly from Beijing." He said he was happy the official had given us "practically the whole morning," when usually they didn't see anybody at all. But I knew Roger was disappointed. He had to be.

So there we were, almost two weeks to the meeting with Mr. Coldwell, and we didn't have one single thing Roger could talk about for longer than five minutes. Not a thing. Roger would only say our plans were not "watertight" yet, and he went on with his usual ways. Since he was no longer working at Taltex, he spent all his hours on the China stuff. He read a lot in the library and ran piles of computer printout on the "projected performances" of the company we were to set up. He was tired and nervous most of the time. Poker Face at the consulate was not returning his calls. And I began to think of being more responsive to my boss at Taltex, at least once in a while, so he wouldn't write me off completely. I was meeting Roger daily after work. He always talked a bunch and was quite upbeat about everything.

In those days, Roger reminded me a lot of a man I'd seen in Las Vegas several years before. I told Roger about it, and he didn't seem to be interested at all. Probably thinking I had no business comparing him with a small-time gambler. It was during one of our night-long meetings. He showed me a thick book of numbers he'd put together for Mr. Coldwell. The book was a result of his many days at the library, and he was quite proud of it. He handed it to me and gave me this look that I was getting very used to at the time. He said, "Well, Eric, Mr. Coldwell should be quite impressed with this. Don't you think?" I told him he looked just like the guy I had seen in Las Vegas. I'd been meaning to tell him that, and it seemed like a perfect time. He just turned away. I never did get to explain what I meant.

Anyway, the guy had on a bright red windbreaker—this man in Las Vegas—and thin, black gloves, and looked kind of dumb at the blackjack table. People were crowding around him because he was apparently having very good luck. His chips were piling up high, and you know how that would get the attention when everyone else was disgusted at how much money they had thrown away. The guy kept winning, and kept raking in the chips. The crowd grew bigger and noisier. When I got up there, he had at least fifteen or twenty stacks of these chips shoulder-high. Then he lost a few rounds and gave back some, which didn't seem to hurt at all. The thing that got everybody was, every time he lost he'd put a lot more back in on the bet, and he'd also raise his head to stare at the dealer for just about half a second. As if he was daring the dealer to take his chips again. Everybody loved it. Pretty soon people were quietly applauding each time he won. And the way he played, when he won, he won big. So this went on for a while. Then the man was finally beginning to lose more and more, you know, every hand having been double or nothing. The crowd was getting testy as hell. You could hear the sighs, boos, and cheers all the way to the other end of the huge casino.

After a few bad rounds, the man moved a mountain of chips forward. He stared at the dealer now for what seemed a whole minute and waited. He still had about half of what he got when he was on top. So everyone thought if he lost, he would walk off, still with a lot of money. If he won, I thought the casino was going to close the table. I could see the security guards and the managers gathering around us.

Things went quicker and quicker. He lost the hand. And without even stopping to think about it, he pushed forward the rest of his chips. Everything. And in a few seconds, he lost them all. The end. The crowd couldn't believe it. They were even more disgusted than they'd been in the first place.

As the guy was playing his last hand, with everything on the line and all the chips out of his reach, he gave the dealer the usual stare, then spoke for the first time. "I'm gonna win this time," he said, "right?" He was kind of mumbling, and everyone was so shocked that he hadn't just gotten up and left with half of his winnings that no one paid attention. The dealer didn't even look at him. The guy's face was different then. He was not panicking or anything. And he didn't seem to expect any real response either; surely no one took him seriously. Few people heard him at all. And I felt, at the time, all he wanted was for someone to say, "Yes, you're gonna win." I felt he'd be happy with it, at least for the moment. And he looked as if he was waiting anxiously, too. As if he was searching hard for a yes or a nod from someone, anyone. But all the attention was on the game, not him.

Later, when the dealer reached for the piles of chips, the man suddenly stood up and said, "Wait." The dealer, trained not ever to be distracted, went on as if he had heard nothing. But the security guards, the managers, and the entire crowd froze in a sudden silence. People thought the man was going to make an exciting scene or something. But he simply leaned forward to shake hands with the dealer, and said, "I thank you very much. Good games." Then he turned around and left. The crowd gave out a big collective groan. They couldn't wait to get away from there.

I still remember that face well, when the man said, "I'm gonna win this time, right?"

What I admired most about Roger was his great ability to give *reasons* for how things had turned out. Not excuses—Roger was never petty—but good, strong réasons. Ones he himself could, and always did, believe in. With all his honesty, too. Other people could have doubted those reasons, but they could never discount them. And that's not all. His reasons also gave him more energy, or motivation, if you will, to charge on. Things *happened* to him a lot, and it seemed most were very negative. But he would simply react by giving reasons, to himself and whoever happened to be around, and would end up even more concentrated. On whatever target he was aiming at. And he did this practically all the time, giving his reasons, on big or small occasions, and in good or bad situations.

Most others who knew Roger thought he rationalized too much and too conveniently. I had thought so, too—that is, until our crazy visit to the Houston Chinese consulate made me realize how well his reasons worked for him.

When we'd been planning that visit, Roger had decided to drive to Houston a day early to "have his own time" and to "work on battle plans" for the meeting. He also wanted to have a "strategy session" with me right before our appointment with the officials. He asked for two hours of my time, but I had my work at Taltex and could only get to Houston in time to give him thirty minutes.

The first thing I heard from him, as soon as I got off the plane in Houston, was that I'd not taken the consulate people "seriously enough." "This is a meticulously-planned meeting, you know, on their part," Roger scolded. "By now they'll have everything mapped out, down to the last detail. Down to who will say what and when. There's probably a script written up already, and rehearsed." We were walking as fast as we could through a huge crowd in Hobby Airport. Roger had dressed ready for top-level actions, complete with gold cuff links and tie tack. His silk tie, striped red and black, gave him a young, intelligent look. I only had a black briefcase to show for the occasion. Since I had had to report to Taltex first that morning, I couldn't possibly have worn a suit. There was a carefully-folded blue tie in my briefcase though.

"You can't just *show up*, you know, you have to *prepare*, for God's sake." Roger was nervous, but he did not waste time getting me situated. For the next thirty minutes, ten in his car and twenty in a video arcade, he gave a very fine description of how he'd "conceptualized" the meeting.

The video arcade was the best place we could find for Roger's "face to face." In the neighborhood around the consulate, it was either the arcade or one of the strip joints—and there were four or five of those.

"See how smart the Chinese are?" Roger had explained to me as we were circling the neighborhood before settling on the arcade. "The U.S. government would never have suspected they'd buy property in *this* area. No one could've bugged the buildings before-hand. The Chinese saw something they liked, boom! They signed the contract, moved right in, set up their consulate, before any-one could do anything. Pretty sharp, huh?"

·   ·   ·

According to Roger, "staff personnel" were to greet us at the gate of the consulate at ten-thirty A.M. sharp, the scheduled appointment time. "Possibly a First Secretary or a consul type," Roger said. Roger would shake hands with them, and I was to do likewise only after he had greeted the "entire party" and had introduced me to them. After that we would be led to a reception area for a "first round of tea," where we should talk as little as possible, especially on the subject of this visit, so our "strategic positions" would not be revealed. We should talk about the weather, loudly, so the Chinese could easily join in the conversation—a "common courtesy" among diplomats. After about ten minutes, we would be led to the formal conference area, where the Consul General and his immediate staff should be waiting with their notebooks. Roger would then sit right next to the Consul General in the middle sofa, facing the door, and I should proceed to the sofa to the immediate left. When I sat down, I would see the second-highest official sitting in his sofa facing me. His sofa and mine would be in front of the two side-walls, where mirrors (possibly one-way) would be placed. When all were seated, things should be easy for me. "You only speak when I ask you to," Roger warned. "I'll handle everything."

What stays with me more, in my memory now, is not how different things turned out, but how Roger had projected them. What he saw, and reported, was so sharply in focus, that it, too, somehow *materialized*. Mr. Poker Face was most definitely not the Consul General as Roger had forecasted. I doubt he was even a First Secretary or a consul. He did have the notebook, did sit in the middle sofa, and with Roger they both did face the door. As for the rest, reality changed course on us. Simple as that.

What awaited us when we finally arrived at the consulate, our ears still ringing from the loud arcade music, was but a closed steel gate. We had to search high and low for the doorbell housed in a wooden, mailbox-like cover. We rang several times, giving long intervals between the rings. Roger kept his ear close to the door, as if waiting for someone inside to talk. Finally a man in a white cotton undershirt, with messy hair, opened the door and looked at us with a frown.

"Mmm?" the man said.

"Yes, my name is Roger Holton, and this is Eric Chung. We have a ten-thirty appointment with the Consul General. The meeting has been arranged by a Miss Shen, Shen Ji-Hua." Roger spoke very slowly and politely. I liked the way he threw in Miss Shen's name in Chinese. Nice touch.

"Shen Ji-Hua?" the man asked loudly, apparently understanding the Chinese part.

"Yes, Shen Ji-Hua. Miss Shen arranged the meeting," Roger said. Then the man opened the door wide and waved us in. He closed the gate and led us to a very small room with a small glass coffee table, about four acrylic chairs, an electric fan, and a telephone. One of his trouser legs was rolled up to just below the knee, and he had plastic slippers on his feet. He motioned for Roger and me to sit down, then turned to leave.

"Sir," Roger called at him, "shall we wait here or . . . "

The man turned around and pushed both his hands forward, as if to move us back, then very carefully closed the door. On the coffee table was a magazine, *Beijing Review*, and a copy of a newspaper, *People's Daily*, which was about four days old and was in Chinese only.

A few minutes later, a young woman knocked and entered the room. "Mr. Roger Holton?" she asked.

"Yes. Shen Ji-Hua?" Roger and I both stood up.

"Nice to have met you, Mr. Holton," Miss Shen said in a pleasant voice. Her English was deliberate and slow, as if she were reading from a textbook. She had on a light-gray Mao jacket, a white shirt and long, light-gray pants. "Please sit down," she said.

"Shen Ji-Hua, is the Consul General ready for us?"

"Consul General?" She was surprised. "We have no arrangement with Consul General."

"But . . . Shen Ji-Hua, you or someone else told me on the phone the other day that the Consul General would see us today at ten-thirty. We represent Mr. Malcolm Coldwell."

"No, I don't think so," Miss Shen said calmly. "And please call me Madame Shen."

"Yes, of course, Madame Shen," Roger stuttered. "Maybe . . . maybe it was someone else then. I was told the arrangements had been made. We have prepared for an important discussion with the Consul General," Roger shook his head, "on behalf of Mr. Malcolm Coldwell."

"Maybe so. I will check." Madame Shen picked up the phone. From what she said, in Chinese, I learned that their understanding was that Mr. Coldwell, a "Texas rich man," wanted a visa to go to China and was sending a representative to discuss the matter. What Shen was going to recommend, at this meeting, was for Mr. Coldwell to join a tour with an approved group visa. However, if Mr. Coldwell had relatives in China, then he could get an individual visa for "visiting kinfolks," but that would require the Consul General's approval.

"No appointment. I am sorry," Shen said, still with a good

smile. "But I can make arrangement with another gentleman, if you like." She paused to look at Roger. "Do you like it?" she asked.

"Yes, of course," Roger replied, "Madame Shen."

"What is the nature of your conversation?"

Roger quickly filled her in on why we were there. She listened carefully, then led us to a bigger room.

After Madame Shen had left, while we waited for "another gentleman," who turned out to be Poker Face, I was very embarrassed for Roger. For his having been way off the mark. I felt so awkward I wanted to leave right away. But Roger was deep in thoughts and totally ignored me. Then, suddenly, he turned to me and grinned broadly. His eyes filled with excitement.

"You see how they are testing us, Eric?" Roger beamed knowingly. "The whole thing was set up to see if we were sincere, if we'd just give up easily." He punched my arm with a fist. "Can't you see it?" And without waiting for my answer, he sighed. "That is a lot of trouble they have gone through. A lot. The game is bigger than I thought. Gosh, Eric, this is bigger than *we* thought."

After the meeting in the consulate, as we waited helplessly every day for a letter or a phone call to come, Roger stuck very much to his story about how the "party," after "proper considerations," was going to contact us. He even theorized that Poker Face, though not the Consul General, was more important. "This is like Deng Xiao Ping is more important than Premier Hua Guo Fong," he said. That you couldn't argue with—and still can't, since Deng Xiao Ping is even today the paramount leader and Hua Guo Fong has long been purged. Every few days he would have a new reason for not getting the call. The Bureau of Foreign Economic Relations was still reading the Houston notes. The members of the National Planning Commission were meeting on it. The Ministry of Electrical Energy was getting the paperwork ready. And so on.

Three days before we were to see Mr. Coldwell, Roger got a letter from Professor Zhang. In the letter was an official invitation, issued by the "National Science Committee of People's Republic of China" for Roger to go to Professor Zhang's university for a "friendly" (we found out later that this meant free of charge) demonstration of American solar energy technology. I jumped when Roger told me. I couldn't believe the kind of luck he had. Or genius. Or faith. When he showed me the letter, though, he was not *overjoyed* or anything. There was a very solemn look about him.

"This is amazing, Eric," he said to me. We were in his small living room. The floor in front of the fireplace was totally covered with magazines, newspaper clippings, books, and his notes. Everything was about China. Even the watercolor paintings and photographs on the walls. He sat up straight and picked up a glass of water. "Energy," he pondered. "Solar, hydro, electric, coal, oil . . . You can't begin to see where this is leading to, Eric." Then he slapped his forehead and said, "Gee! The magnitude of this! I wish I could convince Mr. Coldwell the importance of all this. I wish I could communicate better." Then he looked down at the carpet, his feet kicking the papers close by, and sank into a long, serious silence. The room was dark and I could not see his face well, only his white shirt and the glass of water and that he was almost motionless in the corner. I could feel the heavy, almost suffocating sense of responsibility he was putting on himself.

"Good night, Roger," I said and quietly left him.

•　　•　　•

Professor Zhang's letter quickly decided the topic of what we were going to say in the meeting with Mr. Coldwell. Things suddenly became logical and fell nicely in place. Solar energy pointed to electricity. Electricity pointed to consumer electronics, which consisted of countless component parts that China should be able to make, and sell, cheap. So, our proposal was now called "The Development, Manufacturing and Sales of Chinese Electronic Components in the World Market with Exclusive Rights — A Preliminary Proposal." Roger quickly came up with a name, too, for the meeting itself: "Operation: Launch."

"There's no holding us back now," Roger said.

Roger was adamant about arriving early for "Operation: Launch," so we ended up waiting a long time in a huge conference room, sitting in front of a portrait of Mr. Coldwell. The receptionist came in twice to tell us that Mr. Coldwell's secretary had called and that Mr. Coldwell should be ready "in the next minute or so." On the second time, the receptionist stayed a few minutes to point out some rare antique items in the room: the blue-and-white Chinese porcelain screen attached to the wall, the Persian rug, the four-foot-tall identical pair of cloisonné vases, etc. After that we still waited long, and she never returned.

I turned around again and again to study the portrait — there was plenty of time. In the painting, Mr. Coldwell appeared to be in serious thoughts. His lips pressed tightly together, not showing any hint of smile. His eyes were soft blue, though. They looked out from under his heavy silver-white hair, which was bright against a near-black background. The lines on his face were also soft; and with most everything else in the portrait — his sloped shoulders, the suit, his clenched hand, the solid-colored background, the tie, the antique chair he sat in—so solemn and important-looking, the friendliness of his eyes and face seemed to me a little odd and out of place.

Roger took the opportunity to look over all his notes. He did stop to tell me that it could be "very tricky" to "qualify" me, an "unknown," to Mr. Coldwell and his people. That helped very little with the peace of my mind. I was already getting more nervous by the minute about what we were there to do: talking big on something we knew very little about.

When Mr. Coldwell finally came in, fifty-some minutes late, he had his people with him. He looked older than his portrait and more tough-minded. As he walked up to us, his people quickly filling the room, he seemed hurried and fretful. There was a trace of friendliness in his eyes, though. And his white hair was as thick as in the portrait.

Roger shook hands with everyone, patting one or two on the shoulder. To Mr. Coldwell, Roger said, "How're you, sir." As soon as all were seated, Roger started his speech. He began by introducing me to everyone, pointing out my "unique background."

"Here's a young guy who was born and raised in a traditional Chinese culture, and now, further educated in American— electronics and computers, by the way—and with real, hands-on professional training in a top American electronics firm." Roger put a hand on my shoulder. "And now the Washington Chinese contingency is recommending him to us." Roger paused for my credentials to sink in. I had no idea how Roger planned to prove his connection with the Washington contingency (if there was such a "contingency"), let alone mine.

"Mr. Chung would never acknowledge this," Roger continued

with a smile, "but who's to say that he is not being groomed carefully—American technical training, American language and culture, American corporate style—for a very important function in China, ten or twenty years down the road. A pivotal position perhaps?"

I was secretly hoping that no one would bring up the fact that I had not been born in China, had never been to China, and, had I not already left my country, would never have had a chance to go to China. There had been a couple of occasions in the past when the Chinese leaders had gotten so upset that my native island had experienced the distinct possibilities of being "blood-washed" by the Chinese armies. Since 1949 "friendly visitations" between my country and China had always been out of question.

But, Chinese politics were too complicated for the Senior Advisors and Analysts, and with Mr. Coldwell looking at me with approving eyes from the start, there didn't seem any need for a talk about me. Quickly Roger moved to other, and more important, stuff. Throughout the meeting, Mr. Coldwell treated Roger the same way he treated his own people: direct, blunt, and, I might say, a bit abusive. "Cut the crap!" Mr. Coldwell would say to Roger. Or: "Give us a break, make more sense." To me he was nice and polite. He called me "Mr. Chung," asked for my opinions occasionally, and made sure I had something to drink.

Roger surprised me, and everyone else, with his recollection of Chinese economic statistics, names and ranks of various leaders (and there were many), the agriculture numbers, and commercial laws and regulations. None of Mr. Coldwell's lawyers and accountants could ask a question without making themselves sound stupid. There were piles of information, and before you could barely finish reading the top page of one stack, Roger was already quoting numbers from the next.

And when Mr. Coldwell gave his go-ahead, he even borrowed the word from Roger. "Looks good," Mr. Coldwell said, just like that. "Let's say it's a go. Let's *launch* it."

Roger asked for "two or three million to start with," instead of the thirty million he had said. But Mr. Coldwell promised nothing. Only that it "looked interesting enough" for him, and that he would work on "more comprehensive funding" when things got started.

The only real setback in the meeting for Roger was when Mr. Coldwell mentioned he would need to hire a "top-notch guy" to run this new venture. Roger had assumed, I knew, that *he* would be the President. But the moment Mr. Coldwell finished his sentence, Roger responded, his voice sounding of sincere gratitude: "I appreciate that, sir. This would free me up for investigating other China opportunities for you." He looked at everyone but me. "I simply cannot be tied down by the day-to-day stuff."

It didn't seem to me that there were any "close ties" between Mr. Coldwell—or anyone in his group—and Roger. Roger was as much an "outsider" as I was in the meeting. A *useful* outsider. And I couldn't help but feel a little insecure. But it was no time to be suspicious. Not when Roger was eager to call the meeting his "achievement in life."

Two weeks after "Operation: Launch," Roger and I would make the solar energy trip to China on behalf of Mr. Coldwell (and all expenses paid for by Mr. Coldwell). And four weeks after that, we would both be on the Coldwell Electronics International, Inc.

payroll, Roger as the Special Advisor reporting to the President and me as Roger's assistant with the title Manager of China Affairs. Roger would leave his three-and-a-half-month-old unemployment; I would give a two weeks' notice at Taltex and not miss a day's pay.

8. As Children in Lubbock

In Lubbock in 1972, Mr. Gilbert had said to us in a welcoming speech at Texas Tech: "From now on, forget what you know about America. Pretend you know nothing. Pretend you are a child growing up in Lubbock." Mr. Gilbert's title was Director of Admissions for International Students, and he had in his charge all of us, the foreign students. On behalf of the school, year after year, he gave the official, and probably same, words to the new arrivals. We were seated in nicely cushioned theater chairs with fabric-covered arms. The cool, air-conditioned breezes felt especially nice in a late Texas-summer day. I, sitting together with a group from my country, was fascinated with the auditorium facility, with the kind of money the school was willing to spend on the students.

"What you know, or what you think you know, may only confuse you more, believe me," Mr. Gilbert continued. Certainly no one in Lubbock had seen more foreign students getting into more kinds of troubles. "Don't take anything for granted, look beyond the appearances. And always, always remember to call us when you need help." Mr. Gilbert had his office and home phone numbers projected onto the big screen behind him. Then Mr. Gilbert told us about how an Iranian student had "misinterpreted," and gotten himself and his "young lady date" into a "very embarrassing situation," all because he'd thought his date's having dressed braless was an "invitation for intimacy." "It only seems funny now, but let me assure you, at the time there was nothing to laugh about." Mr. Gilbert smiled and concluded his speech. There were a few giggles in the audience, mostly from the girls. Nobody in our corner laughed. With our daily lives still a big challenge, dating was the least of our concern. And if the males among us should, by miracle, go out with a "young lady date," she would have to do more than *that* to give us the idea. Among the foreign students Mr. Gilbert was known as a "kind man with silver hair," but was of very little real help.

Everyone in the audience had arrived in the States for the first time within the previous two months. Everyone was way over his or her head with a new life: campus facts ("'Red Raiders,' not 'Red Bandits,' is the name of the football team"), the denomination of money ("Count, count, and count before you spend"), the measurement of detergent ("If it's still dirty, put more in next time"), what to say when someone said hello ("Y'all means all of you"), how to ask for the different dishes in the cafeteria ("En-Chi-La-Da. Now say it quickly"), how to address the teachers ("If he's a Ph. D., call him Doctor; if he is a professor, call him Professor, if he is neither, call him Professor anyway") . . . And of course, there was the language. English. Our Public Enemy Number One. With this there were many theories. You could read a magazine that wouldn't bore you over and over again (*Playboy*, for instance), until you almost memorized it, then go on to the next issue. You could watch Johnny Carson every night (plus the cartoons on Saturdays and Sundays). You could study a new phrase daily (beginning with the basics such as "No, but I would like to get my hair shampooed") until the time came when you had learned all that could possibly be said by the Americans. The more philosophical types were strongly convinced Time could take care of everything. With their doctrine, you'd stay dumb and idiotic for a period of time (the length of which would differ according to "individual sensitivities"), until one morning the world would "open up" and you'd "understand everything." Then there were those who believed in more creative approaches.

One Friday night, about three weeks after the start of school, Victor came up to me at the library. I could recognize him from a good distance because he had on the same blue jacket he'd worn on the day he met me at the airport. Also, because the library was almost empty. Only foreign students, many from my country, went to the library on Friday and Saturday nights, having nowhere else to go and nothing better to do.

"New students' orientation tonight, you wanna go?" Victor asked. Then he gave me this smile like I'd be stupid if I didn't know to go along. "Everybody's downstairs." Victor pointed at the window. "Everybody" meant George, Edward, Frank, and Tang-I. The five of us stuck to each other on any travel off campus.

"Of course. Yes." By then I'd learned about the private "orientations" students from my country had traditionally given to the yearly newcomers. Basically they'd load up the new arrivals in a big car and drive to a theater on the 9th Street. There they'd watch the X-rated movies, double features, for two or three hours, depending on when the driver had to leave. That was to be a great treat, since back home this kind of movie was illegal. If any of us had been to them at all, it was usually in a small, damp room in the alleys, and a man would start by telling you what to do if there was a police raid.

"These movies are one hundred percent legal," Victor said as I was getting into his car. The others, already waiting, were talking and laughing. They kept their voices low. Victor and I made a total of six. Three in the front, three in the back. Victor kept his car very clean, inside and out. "Police couldn't care less," Victor said. "This is the way with advanced countries."

The first thing we saw, as we drove up to the 9th Street Theater, was the bright neon-lighted ticket booth. A big sign said ADULT MOVIES, $3.50, and another sign, XXX. On the way, Victor had already explained all those Xs meant "Sex." He also said "Texaco" meant "A Texas Company."

"Are you a member?" the lady asked. Tang-I was already at the ticket booth. He smiled at the lady inside it and said hello. The lady had on a chiffon-looking pink dress you could almost see through. She was fortyish and was kind of fat. Tang-I said hello again, not understanding what the lady wanted. Recently Tang-I had been studying the writings on the men's room walls. He had found words that were similar to what he heard in the dorm all along, so nightly he copied them down and reviewed his notes with a dictionary in hand. He claimed he was communicating much better.

"You have to be a member to get in, it's the law," Victor came up and explained. "You pay four-fifty the first time. She'll give you a card to fill out. The next time you only pay three-fifty, because you are already a member."

The lady smiled at us one by one. We all gave her four-fifty each, except Victor. He showed his card and paid only three-fifty. We got several small cards that said "9th Street Theater Membership." There was also a line on the card. We were supposed to write our names above the line before the lady would allow us in. We took out our pens. There was no time to waste.

"Wait a minute," Victor stopped us. "You are not gonna write down your own names, are you?" Victor looked at us like we had all gone crazy.

"You want this kind of place to know your real name?" Victor gave every one of us a harsh stare. He took out his card. We saw "John Suzuki" above the line for the name.

"Oh, okay. I am now Steve Honda then," I said. Quickly, everyone else also came up with a Japanese name. So we had John Suzuki (Victor), Steve Honda (me), Henry Kawasaki (George), Ed Yamamoto (Edward) and Bento Isuzu (Frank). Tang-I's card simply said: "Mr. Toyota."

"As far as these people are concerned, we are just another bunch of Japanese sex maniacs," Victor beamed. The lady winked at Tang-I and said loudly, "All right, all right." We could now see her dress was very short, both her thighs were showing. We rushed into the theater.

Both of the films were not what you'd call the "hard-core" type. They were both probably made in Europe. The actresses were very beautiful. In the first one, there was piano music in the background when the couple was making love. There was no music or anything in the second one. Only dialogue and the moaning sounds. All of us were quite absorbed. Victor too.

During the intermission, to our surprise, the lady in the ticket booth went on the stage and did a strip dance. She put a tape in the cassette player and danced to the music. Rock and roll. She took everything off except her G-string. Compared to the girls in the movies, her body was not good to look at. Of course she was also much older. We gave her our total attention, though. When she finished we gave her a very good round of applause.

During the second film, the lady came in again. With hot chocolate and coffee on a tray. None of us wanted to buy any. She kept going back and forth. "Try it, you'll like it!" she said half-jokingly. That was what the man in the movie was saying to a blond girl with an incredible body. "Try it, you'll like it," he said with a husky voice.

"Try it, you'll like it," the ticket-booth lady said in her pink outfit. She was much louder, and she held a cup of hot chocolate high in her right hand.

The fact was, we were not "children in Lubbock." We'd all have loved to be, so we could start things over like Mr. Gilbert had said, if it could be that simple. But a child in Lubbock did not have to attend graduate classes. A child in Lubbock would not have been born with a head already filled with a different language. A child in Lubbock would not be deported for "falling out of status." A child in Lubbock learned things that were *new*. We did too, but more importantly, we had to learn how things were *different*. And that, I believe, was the harder part. The part where Mr. Gilbert's theory did not apply. For each of the millions of whys and whats that we had gotten answers for before, we now needed new answers. Quick. The newspaper had twenty times more pages here because there was freedom of speech. People said hello to each other on the streets because Lubbock was only a small town. Students did not rise in the classroom for the professors because everyone was equal in this country. The press could openly attack President Nixon because CIA was actually running the government, and CIA didn't like Nixon anymore. . . .

We knew we must have our new answers. Otherwise we could not survive.

One night, the Pizza Inn on University Avenue was robbed. George, a waiter, and the night manager were the only ones there when two gunmen came in. George had been working there as a part-time busboy for about month. No one was hurt or anything, though the night manager had gotten a hard kick in his back. When Victor and I got there—Mr. Gilbert had called us after receiving a call from the police—there were police cars all over the place; blue and red lights flashed in the darkness. The two gunmen had been gone long before the police arrived. We saw many people going in and out of Pizza Inn. We saw Mr. Gilbert in a phone booth. Two others from my country, Judy Wu and Helen Cheng, were there, too. They were to give George a ride back to the dorm. When we asked about George, the girls only pointed to a window. And we saw, through the window, George talking while a policeman wrote in a notebook. We saw George taken to different corners of the store. We saw George struggling to talk, and using much of his hands and body. We saw George lying on the floor, reenacting the scene, with both hands clasped behind the back of his head and his stomach on the dirty carpet. We saw George point a finger at his temple, simulating a gun. There was nothing for us to do but watch. And the girls were soon sobbing and sniffling. Mr. Gilbert came over and asked us to leave. "Go home before you all freeze to death," he said. Then he told Victor, "Everyone working off campus needs a permit, you know. The school cannot take this kind of responsibility."

The four of us stood in cold wind and watched for about one more hour, until George came out. Then Victor and I took him home. In the car none of us said a word about the incident. George was very shook up, and Victor was in a hard silence. Victor was also driving too fast, almost recklessly. I began to say something about it but soon stopped because he wasn't listening. To Victor, George and the bunch of us were very much his personal responsibility. I could see how he'd gotten *angry* about the armed robbery—George's life could have been lost. And how his anger could have hurt him deeply. Good old Victor.

A few days after the Pizza Inn incident, I was coming out of the bank when a young man about twenty approached me. He politely asked if I was going back to Texas Tech, and if so, if I'd like a ride. "I also go to Tech," he said. It was only about a thirty-minute walk, but the cold weather made him savior of the moment, and I gladly climbed in his car. When we turned in the back side of Sneed Hall, with the street traffic totally blocked, the young man said, "Here you are, sir. Ten dollars, please."

I was planning to give him a dollar for the gas, but didn't expect he would ask that much. I complained about the amount in a friendly way.

The young man looked at me sternly. "Sir, I don't want any trouble. I only want what my service is worth. All I ask is twenty dollars."

"Twenty! But, but you said ten . . . " I tried, desperately, to read his face, now very pale and serious. All my muscles tightened. The thought of opening the car door and running for my life flashed by, but I didn't dare make a move.

"Sir." The young man became rude and anxious. "Like I said. I don't want any trouble. All I want is *thirty* dollars." Then he gazed at me coldly. I quickly took out my money and gave him thirty, leaving me with only five. As soon as he left, I went up to my room, washed my face, hands, and feet with very hot water, then I sat on my bed and stared at the white walls for the rest of the afternoon. First thing next morning, I headed back to the bank for more money.

When Victor knew about my thirty dollars, through my report at the foreign students' office, he became really upset and yelled at me for the longest time, his face turning dark and all that, for not asking him for the ride. Other than that, we—Victor, George, I, and the rest of the gang—didn't talk about this event, either. Like the Pizza Inn thing, somehow we just didn't want to talk about it then. As a matter of fact, we didn't mention the two incidents until about two months later, after we got over the final exams, Christmas holiday, and the beginning of a new semester. And we only sort of joked about it, mainly because George was beginning to brag. Victor never would participate in this, period.

For us, the first-year students, the completion of one semester gave us a great boost in morale. The coming of spring, too, brought certain cheerfulness in our usually narrow and concentrated existences. We began to appreciate the beauty, and quietness, of Texas Tech campus in late March; and in late April, we talked about going to Las Vegas or Ruidoso during summer to earn the next year's tuition. English was still a very serious trouble with us, along with many other problems. But we were relieved that we could prevail despite all. We digested the bus schedule for the trips to downtown. And we "borrowed" a pushcart to transport groceries back to our dorms. And yes, we also began to talk about girls, a lot.

As for the children in Lubbock, we thought they were well-dressed and had angel-like faces. And we wouldn't want for them to live our lives. Ever.

9. THE GREAT WALL

WHEN ROGER AND I ARRIVED in Beijing, China, for the
"friendly" (free) discussions of American solar energy technology
—this was only two weeks after "Operation: Launch"—we had
no idea how to get the "exclusive franchise" for the sales of Chinese electronics. We'd told Mr. Coldwell and his people at
"Operation: Launch" that the Chinese were "receptive" to an
exclusive arrangement, and the solar energy thing was just a way
for both sides to "warm up" to the final phase of negotiations. Mr.
Coldwell had been quite impressed with our report, "The Development, Manufacturing and Sales of Chinese Electronic Components in World Markets with Exclusive Rights—A Preliminary
Proposal" and had given it the go-ahead. During "Operation:
Launch," even with his stacks of data sheets, Roger had managed
to show—and emphasized—the U.S. sales figures of *Japanese*
electronics, year by year from Day One. He'd discounted these
figures for the sake of being conservative, and used them quite
convincingly as our sales projections for China. The same numbers were to become, later, the basis of a five-year business forecast
in the first Board of Directors' meeting of Coldwell Electronics
International, Inc.

We were met at the Beijing International Airport by a man in blue Mao jacket and blue pants. He greeted us with a big smile. While we waited one and a half hours for our luggage, the man kept a smile on his face. He knew very little English. But when I spoke Chinese to him, he didn't say much either. His smile, though, was infectious. Pretty soon he got Roger and me smiling a lot at him, too. There were many people in uniforms at the airport.

My first thought was, it's a different world. My second thought was, it's a world I don't want to live in.

Roger asked a few questions at first, but the man didn't quite respond, so Roger mumbled to himself for a while, then became as nice and quiet as the man. We were put in the Friendship Hotel. The man saw both of us to our rooms, then he said goodbye. Roger wanted me to get his name. The man turned and said, "Mr. Hu," before I could ask. Roger said it was all "very Russian." The rooms had tall ceilings and bare walls, and the towels were old and smelly.

The next morning at eight Mr. Hu showed up and took us in a car to another building, about three miles away at a university campus, which Roger also called "very Russian." We were taken to a room with a big blackboard and filled with people. There was plenty of talking and smoking until we showed up. Then everyone clapped. We had no clues as to what was happening. Everyone was in a gray, blue, or green Mao jacket. We did not know who they were. We were seated in the center on one side of a long table with the blackboard behind us. Three or four people, not including Mr. Hu, sat with us. The rest of the crowd, about forty to fifty, sat in rows facing us. While tea was being served, Roger whispered to me that he could not find Professor Zhang in the room. We sat there watching our tea for a good five minutes before the two men sitting next to Roger stood up.

One of the two men was obviously the leader. The other was the translator. The leader, introduced to us as Mr. Lin, Director of Second Bureau of National Science Committee, took at least ten minutes to say how happy he was to see us there and how long his colleagues had been waiting for our arrival. He then took another ten to describe the places in Beijing that he had "happily" arranged for us to see. "The most special is the Great Wall," Mr. Lin summarized. "According to a Chinese saying, you are not a hero unless you've been to the Great Wall. We will make you both heroes while you are here." Mr. Lin smiled, so did everyone in his group.

"We'll certainly be honored," Roger responded graciously. "No one appreciates the friendship of Chinese people more than we do. But we are not here to be heros. We've come to participate in your Four Modernizations. We've come to work with you."

"Very good." Mr. Lin nodded. Under his leadership, everyone applauded.

Then, as Mr. Lin introduced the group one by one, I began to realize that these were scientists and engineers gathered to hear reports on the "state of the art" solar energy technology in the United States. We were expected to pour onto them all kinds of "advanced information" on a "friendly" (free) basis. We were to use the room for the next four mornings. In the afternoons we were to sightsee. "Everything has been prepared," Mr. Lin said proudly. He leaned toward Roger and asked, "Is my arrangement satisfactory for you?"

"Of course, wonderful," Roger said after sipping his tea. "We look forward to a most successful exchange of ideas." And all

Roger had with him were advertising brochures from about half a dozen companies that made some kind of "solar-driven systems." One company had given us a bunch of miniature solar fans to give to the Chinese as souvenirs. The fans only worked in bright sunlight or under a big lamp.

By the time Mr. Lin finished introducing everyone from "National Science Committee," "Beijing Solar Energy Research Institute," "Ministry of Electronics Industry," "Qinghua University," and "Tianjin Solar Energy Research Institute," the morning was almost gone. We were driven back to our hotel to "rest" for two hours, then another car took us to the Great Wall.

I wasted no time in telling Roger what big trouble we, especially he, had gotten ourselves in, and suggested we make arrangements to leave the next day and forget the whole thing. He insisted there had been some misunderstandings and didn't say much more. Our car traveled through a sea of bicycles to and from the Great Wall. We saw rundown houses by open ditches. We saw horse-drawn wagons piled high with vegetables. We saw people with clothes that looked old and unwashed. We saw many other things that you would call "backward." But everything seemed to give you a strange sense of distance. You could almost get the feeling you were looking down from a higher place. And, however unpleasant things might appear around you, they did not touch your life at all. Not a bit.

In the evening, Roger and I spent hours reading the six advertising brochures over and over again.

The next morning—with still no sign of Professor Zhang—as Roger began to recite his first advertising brochure, I was pleasantly surprised by the kind of attention the Chinese were giving to Roger. The translator gave a fairly adequate version of what was said in English. Everyone was taking long notes. There were private discussions and one or two questions, but overall the whole crowd was very quiet. Roger did try to stretch his stuff as much as he could, but he still ran out of things to say (he'd planned only two brochures a day). The leader, Mr. Lin, gratefully concluded the meeting with everyone applauding Roger. Then off we went, to the Temple of Heaven, for another round of sightseeing.

The following day went pretty much the same way. And the next. While we still did not know how in the world we were going to get someone to sit down with us on the sales of Chinese electronics, we began to like the situation better. Roger even quit looking for Professor Zhang. We became good at blowing the tea leaves away before we drank the tea. We also got used to the cockroaches in the hotel rooms. The waitresses in the hotel restaurant began to recognize us, too, and we learned how to call them—by the identification numbers pinned above the right pockets of their uniforms. We remembered some of the numbers too. 711 was the pretty one. 814 was the one who spoke some English. 744 never paid attention so you should never call her. We also took long walks, after dinners, in the streets and alleys of the city.

On the next to last day of our stay in Beijing, Roger was, even to the Chinese, clearly out of things to say. We were scheduled to visit at least one more "ancient pagoda" than we really wanted, and different dishes at the hotel restaurant were beginning to taste very much the same. Around noon that day a man by the name of Chen Wei stopped in to see us.

Chen Wei, a skinny, balding man in his late thirties, introduced himself as the Manager of the Third Export Division of Components of China People's Electronics Import & Export Corporation. He had received a call from Professor Zhang, he said, and was asked to come see us. "The export of our products," he said, "is very important. Most important." Chen's English was slow and barely understandable. "You see, we need foreign money."

"That's wonderful," Roger said. I could see he was surprised but relieved. So was I. "We have so much to talk about."

"So," Chen said, "first, what do you want to buy and how much do you want to buy?"

"No, no," Roger waved his hand. "We are not here to buy things . . . not yet. We are here to talk about cooperations, joint ventures. . . . "

"Cooperations?" Chen asked. "I don't understand. Please explain."

"Well, first of all, I apologize for not explaining well to Professor Zhang. We were in a hurry to come over here, so I didn't have time to write long letters," Roger hurriedly explained. We were sitting in the first floor coffee shop of the hotel. There were tourists in T-shirts and shorts walking around us, looking at the small souvenirs at the counters. "What we want is a long-term relationship with you. What—by the way, please say hello to Professor Zhang for us, we have not seen him . . . "

"Professor Zhang is very busy man," Chen said calmly.

"I understand," Roger smiled and went back to his pitch. "We represent a man by the name of Malcolm Coldwell. Mr. Coldwell is a very important businessman in the United States." Roger looked up to see Chen. Chen pulled out a notebook and began writing. "He, Mr. Coldwell, is big, wealthy, rich, a lot of money. Very influential . . . "

"Influential? I don't understand. Please explain. And please speak it slowly."

"Okay, okay. A man in the United States, my country, Mr. Malcolm Coldwell, wants to build a permanent business relationship with you."

"Yes?"

"Yes. This man is very important, he has a lot of money."

"Yes?"

"Yes. And we, Eric and I, represent him. He wants to start doing business with you as soon as possible."

"Yes?"

"Yes." Roger was happy with the progress he had made. More tourists came in the coffee shop area to look at things. Roger had to raise his voice a little. "The way he, Mr. Coldwell, wants to do business with you is this . . . "

"Please. Just a minute. What is this man's name?"

"Mr. Coldwell. C-O-L-D-W-E-L-L. Coldwell."

"Thank you," Chen smiled gratefully. "What does he want to buy?" Chen waited eagerly with pen and notebook in his hands.

"All right. This is not gonna work, Eric." Roger turned to me. He didn't lower his voice. "See what you can do to make our amigo here understand."

I took over and told Chen what we basically wanted was to have the rights to sell his products on an exclusive basis. When Chen asked why, I gave him all he'd ever wanted to hear and more about Mr. Coldwell. After I was through, Chen took at least ten minutes to make markings on the notes he had taken. The three of us sat at a small square table. It was getting hot because the window air conditioner could not handle so many people in the room. The tourists, some of them Americans, were joking and hollering about with beers and Chinese soft drinks in hand. You could see the powdery sediment at the bottom of their Chinese soft drinks.

The sediment churned and melted into the liquid when they raised the bottles to drink from them.

"We will consider," Chen said.

"What does that mean?" Roger asked me.

"I don't know," I said.

Chen stood up and wished us a good trip home. When Roger asked that he stay for dinner, Chen didn't accept. Then Roger asked anxiously, "Is there a possibility we could see someone in your organization who can make a decision?"

Chen looked at me. I explained we would like to have an answer before we left. Chen looked very troubled. He frowned, turned away and began to think. After a while, he said, "I think my leaders are very busy. Maybe when you come to China next time . . . "

"Can you at least give it a try?" Roger demanded. Chen looked at me again. I told him it might be considered "impolite" and "unfriendly" to refuse Roger, because, after all, we had traveled a long way to his country. Chen hesitated, then excused himself to make phone calls. A few minutes later, he told us that one of his leaders, Madame Li, could see us the next morning at ten at their corporation office.

"That's great! We leave in the afternoon anyway." Roger was pleased. "Thank you very much, Chen." Roger grabbed Chen's hand and shook it for a while. Later that evening Roger asked me if he should give Chen a camera as a gift of appreciation. I thought about it and told him no.

The next morning, a woman with cropped hair and grand-motherly manners was introduced to us as Madame Li Yuan, Division Manager of the Third Export Division of Components.

She was with seven or eight people. They had been sitting on long sofas wrapped in khaki cloth and drinking their teas when we arrived. The company, China People's Electronics Import & Export Corporation was located in a huge government building. There were guards in military uniforms at the gate.

The people with Madame Li, including Chen, were all part of the same corporation. Three or four of them worked for Madame Li. One was from the Planning Division. Another one was from the Financial Division. They called a short man with a mustache —Mr. Shu—simply a "lawyer."

There was the welcome speech and the presentation of tea, pretty much like what we'd had at the National Science Committee. Roger gracefully accepted and thanked Madame Li. This was followed by the introductions, also like what we'd had before. Then Madame Li insisted everyone drink a sip of tea.

"We are so happy to have you here." Madam Li spoke through an interpreter. She was at ease and attentive, like speaking with an old friend.

"Thank you," Roger nodded.

"Especially you bring good intentions to do business with us. It's like what we Chinese say, 'A friend comes from afar.'"

"Thank you."

"So, Mr. Holton. What do you want to buy?"

10. Training

"What do you want to buy?" the check-out girl at the Furr's Supermarket in Lubbock asked. "Are you sure this is what you want?" The girl picked up a box from our shopping cart. She was about sixteen or seventeen, had a soft, flawless face. Her unaffected ways of showing her concern relieved much of our tensions from the afternoon's shopping. Earlier she had taken back, with smiles and good spirit, a big can of shortening because Tang-I had thought it was a can of chicken meat. The label on the can did show a big chicken, already cooked golden, and the price was a bargain, for a chicken. Aware of his deficiency, and that of the rest of us, Tang-I had, as the girl was ringing up the shortening, asked about the content.

"Chicken?" Tang-I asked, pointing at the can.

"Yes," the girl said, "very good for chicken. And other meats, too." The girl smiled, having gotten used to our asking about what was contained in the packages.

"Good . . . ?" Tang-I was unsure. "No, no, no. Chicken in there?"

"No. No chicken in there. Only shortening." The girl waved and pointed at the can.

"Oh . . . " Tang-I looked as if he had just broken the huge glass window at the supermarket.

"It's all right, no problem." The girl was quick to come to the rescue. "I'll take it back." She skillfully punched on the cash register. I liked the way she said "no problem." Frank and George were snickering. Tang-I gave them a genuine cold eye.

Tang-I, Frank, George, and I were at the supermarket as part of the "exercises" Victor had said we needed very much. In Victor's eyes, our lives were "too small." Victor especially disliked our so-called "five-point way": library, classrooms, dorms, post office, and bank, with the first three taking up ninety-five percent of the time. Victor called this "Chinatown living." "You only speak to each other, in Chinese, in the dorms. And you're too afraid to go outside," Victor had said, pointing to a tree on the campus.

On weekends, when our American friends came back drunk and unconscious, we never thought of them as having good times, and even if we did, we would never have thought of joining in. Life seemed to progress steadily for us, although slow and awkwardly, if we only did the same few things day after day. Any venturing out, we all seemed to fear, might disrupt the whole scheme. And, we rationalized, life isolated us not by our own choice: it had tended to push us back, firmly, whenever we had strayed from our narrow courses. I remember walking twenty-five minutes to buy my first box of detergent, and coming back empty-handed, perplexed by the many brands. I remember giving my oral presentation in class, spending all my courage before the end, and being not able to finish. I remember staring at sixty-odd pages of assigned reading at midnight, having finished only three. You retreat a lot when you get whipped for advances, and you learn to see the merits of staying put. That's why Victor was such a hero. The rest of us only wanted to wait and see, to survive. Victor couldn't stand being cornered. He wanted to succeed.

The most Victor could get us to do, in the first semester, and most of the second, was to work off campus as dishwashers or something, fifteen to twenty hours a week. Our world didn't exactly expand all that much, but we liked the money part. We also tried, as Victor had suggested, sitting down at lunches with some Texas kids, listening to their wild stories which we couldn't possibly understand. After a few days they simply avoided us. While we had the highest regard for Victor, his idea of "jumping into the melting pot" had sounded pretty much a luxury we couldn't afford. But when news came near the end of the second semester that Victor had gotten a job at Petrochem, at $13,000 to start with, we quickly saw the light. For the first time we saw the big pay-off: a real American job with a real American future. A successful exchange of hard labor for rewards. A blueprint for our "way out." This was really what we were after anyway: to become *usable* in this society of abundance, and share in the abundance. We never wanted to go back to our country. That would be a failure, a cop-out. We just hadn't figured out how we could go forward here in the States. Now Victor had a job. We *all* were ecstatic. And more, we wanted to know how we, too, could *succeed*.

"I am not sure this is what you want, sir," the girl said again, urging a response from Tang-I. She raised the box higher so we all could see. Tang-I took a closer look. It was an attractive package with multicolored designs. The word "napkins" was clearly visible.

"Yes, napkin. I want napkin," Tang-I said in defense. He had studied the box before picking it up.

"But . . . these are not paper napkins, sir. These are feminine napkins. They are for ladies," the girl said earnestly. Confused, Tang-I turned to talk to all of us in Chinese. Our line was getting longer. People behind us, seeing four foreign students in a huddle, began to get curious. Either Frank or George quickly figured out the situation and told Tang-I. Tang-I was not embarrassed or anything.

"We still need napkins. You wait here, I'll go find a box." Tang-I pointed at the shopping list Victor had prepared.

"Just forget it!" the rest of us said at almost the same time.

"Okay . . . " Tang-I said to the girl with a forced smile. "This box. Put back. Next time."

"Sure, sir." The girl sounded as if she were talking to her own kid brother. "Next time." She picked up other items from the cart.

When we walked out of the supermarket, Tang-I was still complaining about missing items on the list. "Oh, shut up," George said, giving Tang-I a push from behind. It was about four in the afternoon. We were supposed to have been at Victor's house at three to start making dinner. We got on a bus, each of us carrying a sack of groceries. George also had a six-pack of Cokes. We had to change buses once, and there was a long wait for the connection. By the time we got to Victor's it was almost five.

"Miss Blake will be here in one hour!" Victor said as he opened the door. Miss Blake, the dinner guest, worked for Mr. Gilbert as one of the foreign student counselors. She had a good heart and had become quite familiar to all of us. "Eric in the kitchen with me," Victor said as he began to assign work. His hair was well combed for the evening, and he'd put on a new light-blue shirt with a tall collar. "George and Tang-I, clean the bathroom and living room. I want the bathtub scrubbed, too. Pick up the dead bugs, I've just sprayed. And don't waste more time!" Victor took the grocery sacks from George and Tang-I and pushed the two into the bathroom.

The dinner was part our "training," part Victor's farewell to Miss Blake. Victor was to leave for Petrochem in Houston in about six weeks. The Petrochem job had made Victor the most sought after among the Chinese students. Many, especially the four of us, had repeatedly asked for his helpful hints. Particularly on how to get a job. And Victor had never been stingy about sharing his secrets. "The most important is to Americanize," Victor had said. "You think American, eat American, and live American. Remember, only Americans succeed in this society because, after all, this is an American society." Victor had a wide and flat nose, but we noticed that with his high cheekbones, his deep-set clear eyes, and his hair naturally curly, he did have the profile of some Americans. More or less.

The dinner for Miss Blake, for instance, was to help with the social skills, important for future business life. Victor also had demanded, now that we all had surrendered to his teachings, that we study all the sports pages, memorizing *every* set of scores, and practice telling jokes. "You'll thank me for this," he'd said, "someday." He'd also run a mock interview for the four of us, at our request, with him playing the interviewer and us the job applicants. We used the small conference room in the library for this. Victor was on a sofa. The four of us sat in a row of chairs facing him. We first asked for a minute-by-minute account of Victor's job interviews, though we had heard it all before. This led to Victor's giving us the "guidelines," like what to wear, how to be aggressive, when or whether to show the school transcripts, and how to work in the sports news, or a joke to "make friends" with the interviewers, and so on. Then Victor turned the table on us. "Now tell me, every one of you, why should you be hired?" he challenged. "Pretend I am a Petrochem interviewer. Look me in the eyes. Tell me why you should be hired." Victor sat up and stared at us. "Well? George, why should I hire you?"

"Because, sir . . . " George was surprised at the change of event, but he quickly replied with respect. "I have good background. I get straight A's in my school, and—"

"Not good enough," Victor cut him off. He pushed his sofa back, stood up, and looked down at us. His round chin and the sides of his long, narrow face were much more clean-shaven than before, now that he was about to begin a professional job. "Very boring. I need to know why you are different. Why you are better." Then Victor called on Tang-I. "How about you, Tom?" Victor had said no one could ever remember a name like Tang-I.

"Well, because, sir, I work very hard for you. And I have straight A's too."

Victor shook his head and looked disgusted. He turned his back toward us. "Frank?"

"Well, sir . . . " Frank stuttered. "No. Okay . . . well, because, sir . . . " Frank stopped to think.

"Well?" Victor pushed.

"Well, because, sir, I'll work hard." Frank looked earnestly at Victor. He was tensed up.

"More," Victor raised his voice. He strode quickly toward Frank and punched the back of Frank's chair with a fist. "You've got to say more, all of you," Victor admonished. "The way you talk, the interview will be over in five minutes. You think they'll hire you if they can't get to know you? Tell them something interesting, tell them more about you. Let them know you. If they don't know you, how can they like you? If they don't like you, how can they hire you? Try again, Frank. Don't give me just a few words."

"Okay . . . " Frank collected himself. Sweat showed on his forehead. He thought for about three minutes and said, "Okay let me try . . . "

"Why should I hire you?" Victor led off.

"Well, because, sir, I'll work hard to make money for you . . . " Frank muttered.

"And?"

"And, and how about Cowboys and Redskins, 42 to 30. Third quarter 18 to 21. Two touchdowns last minute. How about it?"

At five-thirty Victor and I had about three dishes ready for the dinner: Shrimp with Cashew Nuts, Kung-Pao Chicken and Two-Flavored Fish. Frank was working hard on the cold plate which involved the thousand-year eggs. George and Tang-I finished the living room area. They had given up on the bathtub. "The bathtub is beyond hope," they said.

"But you've got to have a clean bathroom," Victor said. "That's rule number one in entertaining."

"The bathroom *is* clean. We killed more cockroaches. The bathtub may be a little dirty. But who cares?" Tang-I was a little impatient. "You think Miss Blake is going to take a bath in there?"

"Who knows, she might." Victor raised his eyebrows. "You are just lazy." Victor rented the house with three other graduate students, splitting the hundred-dollar rent four ways. It was a small house supported by four concrete blocks beneath the four corners of the house. There were big empty spaces below the floor of the house and between the concrete blocks. A small child could crawl in and out easily. And could get himself very dirty and smelly. The house was old and falling apart. There was practically no wallpaper left, but the shag carpet was still in fair condition. The plumbing froze up in winters, and all faucets were leaking. The students had been using the house only to sleep, and not very much else. Only two out of four gas burners in the kitchen still worked. And the bathroom, only one, was a sad sight. The walls, the washbasin, the commode, the bathtub, anything originally white, was now yellow to light brown. There was a long crack on the floor, too. The house was ten times worse than the dorm, but it was more than ten times cheaper. Dinner was to be served on a card table, which would normally seat four. The way we had planned it, Miss Blake and Victor would each take one side of the table. Tang-I and I were to sit on a piano bench, sharing another side, and George and Frank the remaining one. They, George and Frank, would sit on the back of an old long sofa. The ceramic and plastic plates were all used up for the food, so everyone, including Miss Blake, had to use paper plates. For the utensils, there were plastic forks. And since we did not bring back the "napkins," a small fold of toilet tissue was placed at each setting—the only substitute we could find in the house. We did bring back a few carnations from the supermarket. They, in the tall drinking glass, did look very nice.

Miss Blake arrived on time at six. Victor still had his apron on, and my hands were still greasy with the kitchen work. But we quickly sat down anyway and started our dinner. Miss Blake was in very good spirit that night. She wore a peach skirt, a short-sleeved white sweater and looked just great with the carnations in front of her. She was about thirty-five and had been working for the International Office since her graduation from Texas Tech. Without our asking, she immediately picked up the fork and reached for the shrimp dish. She had attended enough of these *social occasions* to know exactly what to do. Instantly she praised us on the taste of the food, on the carnations. And she used the toilet tissue without hesitation. The beginning conversation was mostly exchanges between Victor and Miss Blake. Victor's English was not fluent, but he didn't clam up because of it. On the contrary, he tried hard not to stop, speaking whatever came to his mind. Miss Blake patiently listened, nodding once in a while to give him support. When Miss Blake had understood a point Victor was trying to make, she showed her pleasure in a way that was very comforting to us, especially Victor. All four of us listened intently to every word said, as if we were watching a good play. The two-person dialogue continued until we were almost ready for dessert (Almond Bean Curd with Fruit Bits). Miss Blake suddenly turned to us and said: "Victor, are these gentlemen going to sit here all night long without saying a word?" She smiled broadly.

"No," Victor said hastily. "Of course they will speak. That's why they are here. To be social with you. Now I am going to shut up, and they will talk." With that he simply stopped. But no one picked up the conversation for a while. The pressure mounted for the four of us to talk. Miss Blake waited. "Well . . ." I said, seeing that there were no volunteers.

"Yes?" Miss Blake said.

"Miss Blake, your first name is Sherry . . . " I said, my throat tightening.

"Yes, I believe it is. At least the last time I checked." She chuckled, Victor laughed with her.

"There must be other Sherrys . . . right?"

"Right. Many, many."

"How do you tell the difference then. With only the first name. So many Sherrys."

"Well, I don't know." Miss Blake appeared to think about it. "I guess we'd stay confused then, if we only had first names." She and Victor laughed again. I was relieved that I'd done my share of talk. I relaxed and looked at the other three. It was now their turn. There was a long wait again. Finally Frank cleared his throat.

"I am going to tell . . . tell a joke," he said tentatively. Cheap shot. He was going to tell the jokes Victor asked us to memorize.

"That's wonderful. Let's hear it."

"Well, let me think . . . " Frank tried to remember his joke. All of us, except Miss Blake, were getting fidgety.

"Well . . . there is a bridge . . . a bridge . . . game," Frank stuttered.

"Yes, a bridge game. And?"

"One of the men in the bridge . . . game . . . said, 'This game is bad'—no, he said, 'This game is croo . . . crooked.'"

"Yes, the game is crooked." Miss Blake said. "What did the other guys say?" She apparently knew the joke and was trying to give Frank help.

"The other guys said, 'How do you know?'" Frank was getting into it.

"And the man said?"

"The man said, 'That guy is not playing the hand I deal him,'" Frank said, completing his story.

"That's good, Frank," Miss Blake encouraged him. "But you should say 'not playing the cards I *dealt* him,' as in the past tense, not 'deal him.'"

"Not playing the cards I dealt him," Frank repeated with a smile.

"Good. That's a good joke. Right?" Miss Blake looked at us.

"Now who else would like to say something?" There was a longer silence. Victor served the dessert, and everyone lowered his head to eat. No one said a thing.

"OK, I know." Miss Blake raised her voice and said slowly, "How about some football scores?"

"Oh, yes . . . 21 to 10. Steelers and Broncos. Steelers three wins in a row—" George said, jumping right in.

"No, you are wrong. 21 to 7. And 10 to 0. San Francisco and New England." Tang-I didn't wait for George to finish.

"Houston and Minnesota, 16 to 7—"

"31 to 6 San Francisco—"

"34 to 17 . . . "

Miss Blake was the type that made it all seem easy.

11. THE FRONTIERS OF BUSINESS

THE FIRST PRESIDENT OF Coldwell Electronics International, Inc., was Sam Keenes. He, too, had been with Taltex. Mr. Coldwell put out a search for the "best man available in electronics" and found him working at Taltex's Defense Electronics Division as a Strategy Planning Manager, job grade 30. It was right after Roger and Mr. Coldwell's Senior Advisors and Analysts had started all the legal paper on Coldwell Electronics International, Inc., according to Mr. Coldwell's instructions at the "Operation: Launch" meeting. Mr. Coldwell called a few of his friends in town, and one of them happened to be a past chairman of a big bank who had a friend in the electronics business. This friend called a few more friends, and came up with Sam's name. Mr. Coldwell personally called Sam.

Sam was tall and slim. He had a deep, loud voice and always spoke as if he had been asked to give conclusions, as if he was to be the one to finally explain it all so you wouldn't need to ask anymore. I'd say he was greatest when he wanted to convince you. He could really let you have it, good or bad, depending on whether you agreed with him or not. I don't mean to say he'd get ugly or anything. He wouldn't. But you'd tend to feel there was something deeply wrong with you if you didn't see things his way.

Mr. Coldwell was impressed the minute Sam started talking. By the time their first meeting ended, Sam was offered the job as the President of Coldwell Electronics International, Inc. Mr. Coldwell doubled what Sam was making at Taltex.

Sam called Mr. Coldwell back in about a week to accept the position. He also wrote a long letter to make things formal. In the letter he said:

.... The prospect of initiating a commercial enterprise with such potential cannot but instill in one a sense of entrepreneurial spirit which is often lacking in corporate America of the present days. Those who brought the Japanese electronics into this country twenty years ago might have experienced similar challenges. The reward for those who were able to persist and conquer was, as we all have witnessed, unimaginably vast. I thank you for your kind offer, for allowing me to participate in a most exciting adventure, however trying it might prove to be, into the frontiers of business. . . .

In the first Board of Directors meeting at Coldwell Electronics International, Inc., a couple of months after "Operation: Launch," Sam presented to Mr. Coldwell and the Senior Advisors and Analysts a five-year plan. It was basically a way to tell Mr. Coldwell how much money he, Sam Keenes, was going to make for the company. Sam had worked for weeks on the numbers, utilizing the complex "strategic planning models" that he had learned so well at Taltex. But when he released his numbers in a small "dry run" a few of us held in preparation for the Board meeting, Roger immediately noticed that they were almost identical to the set of figures *he* had presented at the "Operation: Launch."

"It all goes back to my original plan," Roger whispered to me while Sam was rehearsing his speech. "They can hire all the high-powered executives they want for the job. It all has to go back to my plan." Roger gave me a nudge. "Right?"

I pretended not to be paying attention. There was no point in encouraging him since his "original plan" had been based on the Japanese sales statistics in the first place.

According to Sam's plan, in 1980, the first year of the company, we were going to lose about $250,000. This was because we'd only got started and you couldn't really expect any miracles yet (we lost over $400,000 that year). In 1981, we were to "break even" and begin to make "a small profit," say in the neighborhood of $150,000 (we lost $600,000). And in 1982, the third year of operation, our basic products would begin enjoying "market recognitions" and breaking grounds in "market shares." We would make $1,250,000 ($500,000 in the red). The fourth year, 1983, the year we could "reap the rewards" of the "distributive systems established in the previous three years," we were to continue "our stronghold in the marketplace with basic products," and "further advance our positions with newly developed products of the highest quality." For this year we forecasted profits in the range of $6,000,000 (another $400,000 in the hole). And finally, the fifth year. 1984. Sky's the limit. Everything was to go our way. All our hard labor was to begin to pay off. "Most conservatively," Sam concluded, "the company's profits for the year should be up to $12,000,000" (loss: $400,000).

At the end of the Board meeting, Sam said: "We understand our optimism and enthusiasm may have clouded our visions. But these numbers are in no way exaggerated. What we are saying here is, we will do, in the next five years, all together, the amount of business that is less than one two-thousandths of what is currently being done in the United States in a single year. On products similar to or the same as ours. One two-thousandths. And that's in five years. We think with the talents we have managed to gather here—" Sam looked around at each of the employees at Coldwell Electronics International, Inc., about six with Roger and me included, as well as the Senior Advisors and Analysts, then looked straight at Mr. Coldwell, "we should be able to accomplish that. At least. Or we don't deserve to be here."

At the time Sam was made the President, he was also made a Director. There were a total of six Directors at Coldwell Electronics International, Inc. Mr. Coldwell himself was a Director and the Chairman of the Board. Mr. Coldwell's niece, Carolyn Coldwell, and eldest nephew, William Coldwell, were also Directors. The two remaining Directors were Roger and me.

Sam was entitled to six percent of the stock as soon as the company began to "show profit." Roger and I were to own a total of nine percent (Roger seven and I two) under the same conditions, leaving Mr. Coldwell, his niece Carolyn, and his nephew William with eighty-five percent.

In a legal contract among all the Directors, we called all of us, including Mr. Coldwell's niece and nephew, "founders" of the company.

The first thing Sam did, as soon as his five-year plan had been approved by the Board, was to send Roger and me back to China again. And again. Within four months after the "solar energy demonstration," Roger and I had made three more quick trips to Beijing. We still didn't accomplish much. People in the China People's Electronics Import & Export Corporation, some of them, did finally begin to understand what we meant when we said "exclusive," "cooperation," "worldwide rights," "distributor," and "Mr. Coldwell." But that was all. We had to start the discussion all over each time. If we ever assumed what we'd said before had been understood and remembered, we would only confuse the Chinese more, and end up getting ourselves confused too. It was really something.

All three trips we were put in the Friendship Hotel—the same one as for our very first trip. We got to know the waitresses in the hotel restaurant much better and did not have to wait long for the service. They would bring our drinks—Laoshan mineral water for Roger and orange soda for me—as soon as we sat down at the table, and would recommend dishes for us. We still had to call them by their numbers; it seemed rude for us to ask about their names. Roger and I also ventured out more into the streets after dinners. We stood beside the streets watching people prepare meals outside of their houses with simple mud stoves. We played with the children when they were not afraid of the sight of Roger. And we watched young women practicing walking in high-heeled shoes.

We were convinced that Madame Li, Chen Wei, Mr. Yeh and others of China People's Electronics were serious and earnest, but they knew nothing about the real business world. And we had a feeling that they thought the same about us.

"Chinese minds work very differently," we reported to Sam every time on our return to Dallas. And that was about the only thing of any significance we could say.

A couple more months passed and, impatient with the lack of

progress, Sam joined in and made two additional trips with Roger and me. These two trips were characterized by marathon-styled, hard-hitting, single-focus meetings that Sam had been well-geared for at Taltex. We often kept Chen Wei, Mr. Yeh, and sometimes Madame Li, in our hotel till two or three in the morning, trying with all our might to hammer one thing into their heads: "Let us sell your products on an exclusive basis, and we'll make you as successful as the Japanese." They seemed to have understood well at the end of each session, when they were also faced with the difficult tasks of getting home—the last buses left sharply at twelve midnight, and very few taxi drivers in Beijing worked overtime. But the next day they would ask the same questions again.

We did ultimately emerge from these meetings with a break-through. In the end the Chinese did give us a fifteen-page "Memorandum of Meetings." It was a faithful recording of all our meetings—time, place, and who had said what—with an added small paragraph expressing their "strong intention" to give Cold-well Electronics International, Inc., an exclusive right to sell five products. We had asked for seventy products. Madame Li said more could be added as "our mutual friendship grows old." Madame Li also said that they would not sign a formal contract until they had a chance to visit us in the United States.

"By visiting you we can increase our mutual understanding," Madame Li explained at a small ceremony she held for the sign-ing of the Memorandum. Almost thirty people from China People's Electronics Import & Export Corporation attended the occa-sion, including Madame Li's three superiors. "The more understanding, the better we can work with you."

"That's all very fine," Sam responded. "But come quickly, please."

． ． ．

It took three months for their Ministry of Public Safety to go through "political examinations" on each member of Madame Li's delegation, one more month for the Ministry of Foreign Affairs to issue travel documents, and, finally, "twenty working days" at the American embassy in Beijing to get visas stamped. We waited and waited. We did a lot of "planning meetings," or "brainstorms." Not much in real business could be done without the contract.

To our surprise, when Madame Li's delegation eventually arrived at the DFW International Airport, a quiet, tall man in a long felt coat was introduced to us as "Mr. Huang, Manager of Components Manufacturing," and the "leader of the delegation." We—Sam, Roger, and I—had never met this man before and did not know when he had gotten involved or whether he knew *anything* about the project at all. Mr. Huang was nice and calm, leaving most of the business conversation, and much of everything else to Madame Li, supposedly the second in command. He only talked to us directly once. In a very polite way, he asked us to step aside and "rest" while they grouped and convened in the luggage area.

"Don't be fooled," Roger said to Sam and me. We stood in a corner watching as they scrambled to move their belongings off the luggage carousel. "The real boss is Madame Li. Mr. Huang is really a party functionary. He's been given the manager's title and put in the group to oversee matters of political ramifications." The delegation quickly assembled all their suitcases. Madame Li and Mr. Huang only stood by, not having to do any work.

"You'll see," said Roger. "When they have a question, they'll ask Madame Li, and not Mr. Huang. This Huang guy will drop out of sight soon, if nothing embarrassing happens while they are here, like a defection or something."

Sure enough, after this trip we never saw Mr. Huang again. Madame Li and the rest of the group, Chen Wei, Mr. Shu (lawyer), and Mr. Yeh (of the Planning Division) did later return to the States more than once and became as big a part of our lives as, I am sure, we did theirs. That first trip they were all in their Mao suits when they got off the plane. The Mao suits were not seen again either, except in Chen Wei's case, on their return trips to Dallas.

For first-time visitors of America, those coming from a very different and materially poor society, Madame Li's group seemed quite unimpressed. They were shown all the tall buildings, hotels, warehouses, and different factories that Mr. Coldwell owned (and some Mr. Coldwell did not own). They were wined and dined on top of Reunion Tower, from which they viewed Dallas night traffic for a good three hours. They were at Six Flags one afternoon (because we'd read a *Newsweek* article about Soviet negotiators having a good time at Disneyland), and all of them went on rides. They were driven past, for picture-taking, where President Kennedy had been assassinated.

There was not much business to discuss—they came to sign on something they had agreed to several months before—so we kept showing them around. They thanked us repeatedly for our hospitality, especially after a good Chinese meal, but never said if they liked the food, sights, places, or whatever. Or if they liked anything at all. When asked, Madame Li would say for the group: "We don't know how to repatriate your kindness. Everything is wonderful." With her straight hair cut ear-short and her Mao suit, Madame Li had attracted attention wherever we had been.

When I was doing the driving, I'd stop now and then to point out things that they might not have seen before: shopping malls, new-car dealerships, motels, a soccer game between *uniformed* second graders, the McDonald's, highway intersections (ramp, service roads, overpasses, and all), golf courses, a family in a Winnebago—things that had impressed *me* a long time ago, when I first saw them. I'd take time to explain, too, giving them plenty of opportunity to ask. But they only nodded appreciatively as I spoke, and never requested more information. I became a little frustrated one night and was interested in finding out how they really *felt*. About America. About better things in life.

"Ask me anything," I urged. We were pulling away from a gas station, heading south on I-35 to go back to their hotel. "So I can help you understand America more. Anything." I turned to Mr. Shu and Chen Wei in the back seat. "Even how much money I make."

"How much money do you make?" Madame Li asked, not understanding my humor. I told her anyway, giving myself a twenty percent increase in salary.

"Oh," Madame Li said, showing no emotions.

"That's good," Mr. Shu said. He took out a notebook to write on.

"Are there a lot of robberies and murders in America?" Madame Li asked. "Are some cities not safe to visit?"

"And also about the old people, are they not taken care of?" Chen Wei said, interrupting me before I began to think about murders and robberies. "Please talk about this also. About old people."

"Yes . . . old people. I'll try to explain." My interest in this conversation was quickly diminishing.

"How about the workers? They are fired easily and left to starve?" Mr. Shu asked. "We heard the capitalists here can fire workers at will."

"Another thing is the prices," Madame Li said as soon as Mr. Shu finished. "Do they go up all the time? Without control? And are they all very high now?"

"Some are high, yes," I responded. I was glad there was finally something I could talk about with some dignity. "But not all. The gasoline is about thirty cents per liter. This is not too high." I knew gasoline in China was priced much higher.

"Not bad," Madame Li said. "How about pork . . . ?" And with that we started a long discussion on the prices of different things: eggs, rice, my pen set, my car, my suit, newspaper, Cokes, hair-dos, school tuition, bicycles. . . . Whenever I reported a definite pricing information, Mr. Shu would take note, and Madame Li would do her calculation to see how much that would be in their money. It turned out about half of the items were cheaper here than in China. This was a surprise to them. And to me. But they were not convinced. "We need to get a lot more prices for a good comparison. Can you help us?" Chen Wei asked. We had arrived at their hotel. The three of them, all red-eyed and tired from the jet lag, had no intention of leaving my car. So I took them to a big twenty-four-hour grocery store and let them read price tags until almost eleven-thirty that night.

Everyone at Coldwell Electronics International, Inc., thought this was the funniest, the Chinese having gotten into prices and stuff with me. "What do you expect?" Roger said with mock amazement. "They've been told, all their lives, that theirs is a much better society: less crime, cleaner streets, guaranteed jobs, and even cheaper things. They don't want to be told otherwise by you." Roger said his rides were mostly quiet because he hadn't let his Chinese passengers, Mr. Huang and Mr. Yeh, talk too much.

For the last two days of their stay in the States, the delegation was invited to Mr. Coldwell's 7000-acre, 2000-head cattle ranch in south Texas, about four hours' drive from Dallas. I specifically warned them, before departure, not to ask too many questions on the ranch, especially about what things cost.

Within hours of their arrival, Mr. Yeh of the Planning Division drove a motorcycle into the lake.

None of the Chinese ever asked what Mr. Coldwell, an insurance man, was doing selling electronics. Then, none of us ever asked either, not Roger or Sam, not I, not all those people hired to work at Coldwell Electronics International, Inc., and certainly not the Senior Advisors and Analysts.

Within the first year of business, Sam and the two old marketing hands he hired, Jesse Halstead and John Drew, were able to get some small orders for the five Chinese products. Jesse was about forty and had sold electronic parts for fifteen years. He jogged every day and had a way of frowning at people to let them know they were bothering him. He could also be very humble to his clients if he wanted to. John was a retired Electronics Engineer from a major computer company. He was working to help pay for his daughter's medical bills. He and Jesse often visited the buyers together. Jesse would give the sales pitch and John the technical details. They went on the road for about two months with nicely printed brochures on the five products, and told the buyers how we were "strongly backed" by Mr. Coldwell, and how the Chinese had "contracted" us to "speak for them" exclusively. Most of the orders they brought back ended up in "backlog" files. We spent the following year and half finding out none of the orders were good because:

a. the Chinese could not make the products (even though there were brochures and all that);
b. the Chinese could make the products but could not package them right;
c. the Chinese could make and package them, but could not ship until two years later;
d. the Chinese could make, package, and ship, but they thought the prices we'd sold to the customers were "outrageous" and wanted us to go back and raise the price by 100 percent;
e. making, packaging, shipping, and pricing were "no problems," but in order to produce the quantities we would "eventually require," we would have to invest in a new production line (cost: four to six million).

We spent another eight to nine months learning, by getting more orders, that all five exclusive products, each and every one, had these same problems.

Then we insisted on adding more products to our exclusive right. We figured that China People's Electronics must have given us the harder products to work with first—"start the Westerners on the bitter end" was a known Chinese business practice—and had saved the easier ones, ones with big profit possibilities, as the future reward to be handed out when we managed to prove our worth. And we simply had to get our hands on those easier ones, *now*.

The Chinese resisted, but eventually agreed. We increased from five to ten products. To twenty. Then we worked up to "adding by notification," meaning whatever we wanted, it was exclusively ours—if we only "notified" them. But nothing changed. Same old song, different verses.

During one of the more *emotional* meetings—two years or so after the founding of Coldwell Electronics International, Inc.—with Madame Li and Sam Keenes as heads of two sides, things got so hot Sam pounded on the table, yelled at the Chinese (the exact words were not translated), and stormed out of a conference room in the Coldwell Building. At the time we had been hit by more and more problems with the products, and were determined to get additional ones, on exclusive basis, from China People's Electronics. Either that or we had to shut down. So Sam couldn't possibly take no for an answer. Madame Li, on the other hand, needed to consult with all of her superiors, so she said, on a matter of such importance. Sam was clearly unable to understand. He cursed and slammed the door, and Madame Li immediately complained.

"You can't do business with this kind of attitude," Madame Li said to me in Chinese.

"The attitude has nothing to do with business," I said. "Sam must have new products, or we can only close up and go home."

Madame Li put a hand over her mouth and gave a look of disbelief. "But you *have* things to do, Eric." She deliberately lowered her voice to a friendlier tone. "You have five products. There are problems, I understand, but by working together, all of us, we can eventually find markets for them."

"We don't have five years, Madame Li. My company must make money in five months," I said. But I didn't go into it more. Madame Li obviously didn't know what sorry shape her products were in. And I knew for sure she'd never understand why a rich man like Mr. Coldwell would close up a company.

Two others were in Madame Li's delegation this time: Mr. Shu, the lawyer, and Mr. Yeh of the Planning Division. For all of them, this was either the third or the fourth trip to the States. On the night of their arrival, Madame Li had asked me to get a bottle of "good perfume" for her. I was happy to comply.

"How do we look, have we improved?" she asked the next morning when I picked up the delegation. Both Mr. Shu and Mr. Yeh were in dark suits and white shirts. Their ties were wrinkled from the travel, and their hair was not combed well. Madame Li was in a gray business suit. Her shoes looked dusty and oversized and she had on a pair of short socks.

"Yeah, you look nice. Very American," I said, knowing how serious they were about having the "right image" in Western countries.

"My two comrades—these two gentleman had their suits specially made, by the Ministry of Foreign Affairs only weeks before we came."

"They look wonderful," I said and handed her the perfume.

"Thank you. This perfume is what we need," Madame Li said to me. She removed the cap. And before I could say anything, she sprayed the perfume on the two men, and then on herself. "This way we smell good," she said. "You know," Madame Li glanced at my tie, "there were reports about Chinese delegations not smelling good. They said foreigners don't like our smell."

In the Coldwell Building parking lot, Madame Li took the perfume bottle out again to spray. As we wandered through the corridors of the eighteenth floor in the Coldwell Building to go to the conference room, a cloud of Chanel No. 5 traveled along, with the delegation—and me—very much in it. There were a lot of looks and glances along the way, and a few snickers. And before we went into the conference room, I took it upon myself to stop Madame Li as she made yet another reach for the perfume bottle. "Save some for later," I said. And after greetings and cheerful small talk in the conference room, and before we got serious on the business, Sam whispered, "What did you do, turn them into Avon ladies?"

The one person obviously missing from this trip was Chen Wei. The Chen Wei who introduced us to Madame Li in the first place and had actually started the whole business with Roger and me. Chen had always been around, so it was kind of odd to see the delegation without him. We had liked Chen Wei's straight talk, although he could get stubborn about what he'd called "the Chinese way." Chen Wei had refused to use American legal terms in our agreements. He'd not dressed in Western suits, like everyone else. And even though English had not been a problem for him, he'd insisted on speaking Chinese in all the meetings, despite the fact their translators always messed things up. We didn't like what he'd had us go through sometimes. Like working all night trying to come up with other ways to say "force majeure" or "God's will," but we liked him anyway. Somehow we thought he was honest.

One afternoon during their previous visit to the States, I had taken the delegation to a McDonald's for a late lunch. While everyone else enjoyed the hamburgers, complete with Cokes, ketchup, and french fries, Chen took out a bag containing the lunch he had made for himself that morning. He unwrapped rice, some chicken, dark-looking pickled vegetables, and a banana.

A waitress came over and began explaining the restaurant policy against "outside food." Chen suddenly exploded and was almost shouting at her, in English. "You got your rules and we got ours!" Chen pointed a trembling finger at her. "You live by your rules. We live by our rules. Okay?" The waitress quickly went to a corner to talk to the manager. Madame Li looked very upset, but had nothing to say.

When I went to check on them in the motel that night, as I did with all their visits, making sure they were not harassed or anything, I heard loud yelling coming from Chen Wei's room. I stepped closer and saw through the window Chen sitting in a chair with his head lowered and Madame Li and the others standing about him, lecturing at him in very harsh language. I decided not to get involved and drove away to a restaurant for dinner. When I came back, an hour later, they were still at it. The room was full of cigarette smoke, and Chen's head had sunk into his hands. That was Chen Wei's last trip to America.

Chen Wei's absence did not get much attention from most people at Coldwell Electronics International, Inc. Sam only said, "Well, there goes the Chinese dignity."

"Of course it'll take some time," Madame Li said to me after Sam had stormed out of the meeting. "Everything takes time. You can't get to the top of a mountain in one day."

"All Sam wants is to sell more products for you. Isn't this good for you too? Isn't this why we are all here?"

Madame Li sighed. "I can't make that kind of decision. We are not a Western company. Many people will have to . . . study this. We have to research more."

"But . . . "

"Mr. Chung," Madame Li said, leaning towards me, "China is backward. We have a lot to catch up with, to learn. We need help. Mr. Coldwell can help us. He is very friendly and has the patience." She spoke thoughtfully. "We will not forget him." I didn't have the heart to tell her Mr. Coldwell was not going to like this "friendship" too much longer if he had to put in more money. Madame Li looked very troubled, so did Mr. Shu and Mr. Yeh.

"And Eric, I think of you as a compatriot," Madame Li continued. "You understand our difficulties. You are by blood one of us. You should help us talk to *them*." She looked serious and sincere. Mr. Shu and Mr. Yeh agreed.

"Wait . . . " I suddenly felt isolated by her calling me a "compatriot." "What does all this have to do with business?" None of them responded. I slowly stood up and walked out of the conference room, trying to clear my thoughts.

A few minutes later, Sam and I, as well as Jesse and John, went back to the conference room to resume the meeting. "We might as well see what they can come up with," Sam said.

"Come in, come in," Madame Li said, breaking into a big smile. "Let's sit down and talk." She looked as if she was enjoying the glory of a small conquest—our return to the table. She has her victory, I thought at the time, as long as we will talk to her. Sam was a different story all together: he had to find victory somewhere else.

12. Write: "I Love America"

A COMPATRIOT, MADAME LI called me.

My country is a small ocean island, hit by at least three typhoons a year, colonized twice by different invaders, abundant only in banana trees and rice, and throughout our own history, a logical hiding place for outlaws and defeated generals with remnant troops. All this might help explain why some folks, from way back, have simply packed up and left (and ended up building railroads in other countries). But it probably better explains, with what we've been through and all that, why our people do not trust success. Nowadays newspapers all over the world, seeing how my people can turn out millions of electrical fans for GE and Westinghouse simultaneously, and still have time to build computer parts for AT&T, are saying the island is an economic miracle. What they should say, most likely, is what marvelous things *fear of being wiped out* can make people do. The island's richest hustle for the same thing as the island's poorest: the next buck. And everybody watches out for what others are doing right, so he or she can do *exactly* the same. "It's a society of dogs," my father used to say. This was back when the world still had a problem finding us on the map, let alone calling us any kind of miracle. Back when *everyone* was poor on the island. "We also have very few heroes," my father would say, "but dogs don't eat heroes. Dogs only eat dogs."

My father had a small two-room souvenir shop then; the second room was where we cooked and slept. By the standards of the time, we were doing well. My father was to make what seemed to us a small fortune in the sixties when the Vietnam War brought vacationing American GIs and their Chinese "girlfriends" to our shop. Although apparently hoping his children would someday be clever enough to leave the country for their own good, my father never came out and said so. He did drop the hints though, once in a while, using certain occasions, such as a bloody street fight or a policeman coming around for his monthly bribe, to say, "No, this is not a place to stay." But that was not enough to get us thinking. As children, we caught mice from under the bed and jumped in and out of open ditches for fun.

The typhoons came mostly in late summers and always brought lots of rain. Our city was large, but there was no "underground drainage" to talk about. The result was floods for the part of the city (about one-third) which was on lower grounds. The water would begin to come in the middle of the storm, and keep rising, sometimes to three or four feet, sometimes ten or twelve, until after the typhoon passed, the wind died down, and the rain stopped, leaving thousands of homes in the water for several days.

On the eves of a typhoon my family would sit up all night by the candlelight (electrical power was always the first to go) and watch for signs of the flood. When small streams of dirty rivers began to flow in the house, we would pile chests, tables, and chairs on top of each other. When the water, with dead things and stuff floating in it, came up to the height of the bed, my father would wade to the front door and pull out all the wooden strips he had nailed in earlier as reinforcements. When the water brimmed over the bed, my father would say, "Let's go." And he would take one of the children on his back and begin a dark journey in the rainstorm to a higher point. He would repeat this trip for the remaining two children. When the last trip was made, with the oldest child, me, on his back, the water would be up to his chest and he would have difficulty breathing. He would quicken his pace when he could manage, but would always make sure one foot was solidly on the ground, under the quick-flowing water, before the other was lifted. He would keep his head high and ask me to wipe his eyes so he could fix his sight on the distant landmarks. When we finally arrived at higher ground, my brothers would be waiting, trembling in wet clothes, but would not dare complain.

Hundreds of other families, too, would be there facing a huge lake, seeing their houses disappear in water. My father would put us in a cheap hotel and have us take baths in "boiling hot water." A few days later everyone would return to what was left of their homes. We would help my father scrape dirt off the walls, cabinets, furniture, and various merchandise in the souvenir shop. We would end up throwing most of the things away. The rest would have a strong smell for months. And the city would have plenty of cholera cases. And my father would say to us, "This is not a place to stay."

My father never intended for any of his children to take over the souvenir shop—nothing could have been further in his mind. But he'd never insulate us from it either. As an owner of a small business employing two or three, he was considered doing well. There were always people in and out, customers, vendors, relatives who wanted to borrow money, other shopkeepers, and so on. And those who were worthy of a conference with my father would be invited inside to the bedroom. There they would sit on the bed and be served American coffee and the day's newspaper.

One night a vendor sent a delivery man over with new merchandise. The store was closed then, and the man had to knock to come in. He inadvertently broke the door handle and my father was upset about it. "I'll tell your boss about this," my father threatened.

The man was clearly alarmed. "Oh, please don't. My boss will get angry," he pleaded. But my father wouldn't agree. He told the man to leave immediately and locked the door.

"Please, sir, do not tell my boss. Please," the man again asked. He stood outside by his bicycle.

"Just go back. I'll discuss this with your boss," my father said.

"No, please don't. My boss will fire me." The man was almost crying.

My father didn't respond. And the man kept pleading and begging. Later, when my father simply stopped talking, the man kept saying the same thing over and over.

"Sir, please, spare me this time."

"Sir, please, spare me this time." More and more the man's cry turned into insistent wailing. He kept on for about an hour; his voice was hoarse. My father still would not give in. None of the neighbors said anything—they knew better than to meddle. But my youngest brother was frightened and began to weep quietly. My father then told the man he would call the police. The man reluctantly left, his voice fading away, without any assurances from my father. After that my father said for us to go to sleep. But we tossed and turned for a long time, saddened, not by my father's coldness that night, but by the thought that we might have to go out there too, someday, and like the man, plead and beg for others' small kindnesses.

Life in my country was seldom talked about in Lubbock by me and my expatriate friends. The past was fast becoming very *distant* now that the future, which kept us occupied, was bound to be entirely different. But sooner or later, one way or the other, we got to know, very specifically, about each other's background.

Victor's father had owned a small textile factory and had made very good money until he lost everything on the mah-jongg table. Later he quit gambling, started over, and made a decent living exporting eel-skin wallets to the United States.

When Tang-I was only four, his father was arrested for organizing a political party and was quickly executed. Tang-I did not know about the death until he was in junior high school. The family lived on a stretch of rice field which was later sold to the government, at a good price, as the site of a new refinery.

George's father and mother both taught high school for many years, not even making enough to feed the children. George never owned a pair of new shoes until he was in college, when his parents quit the high school jobs and began giving private classes on how to pass the American college tests like TOEFL, SAT, GRE, GMAT, and so forth. They saw the money grow. After George left, his parents bought a small Toyota and a condominium on the top of a hill.

Frank's father retired from the army, drove a taxi, built roads, worked on a government farm and never had much of a saving.

Frank got a full scholarship from Texas Tech and mailed three hundred dollars a month home.

I took my first English conversation class, during my first high school summer, from an American college student whose father was, at the time, one of the thirty thousand troops stationed in my country. She was eager, kind, and curious about everything. In the first session she wanted an English name for everybody. The students, one by one, came up with a name that they wanted to be called. When it was my turn, I nervously offered my choice, Wayne, after my movie hero John Wayne.

"What?" Miss Linda, our teacher, did not hear me well. "I'm sorry. Can you spell it for me?"

"Yes . . . W. . . eh, W. . . A . . . " I hesitated, my face turning red. "W-A . . . W-A-N-A"

"W-A-N-N-A, is that what you said? W-A-N-N-A?" she asked, smiling kindly.

"Yes . . . " I replied in a low voice.

"OK, that's good, Wanna. Wanna Chung." She nodded and went on to the next in line. And the whole summer long, she called me Wanna. I quickly impressed her with my memorizing, without mistakes, the names of the days in a week and the months. No one else in class could even come close. And when we were on the subject of the calendar, she especially liked to call on me.

"Wanna," Miss Linda would call out with her joyful voice, "what are the seven days of the week?"

"Monday, Tuesday, Wednesday, Thursday, Friday, Saturday, and Sunday," I would say, in one breath.

"That's wonderful, Wanna," she would say. "Marvelous."

At the end of summer, I gave her a small farewell gift from my father's shop. Weeks later, she sent me an article she'd written for her university's newspaper in the States. It was about her experience in my country. In the article, she described me as "an example of the bright, hard-working high school students" she had had in her class. Twenty years later, I would be, like Miss Linda, an American citizen.

I became a citizen of the United States about the time Mary and I were moved down here. There was an exam—the Immigration called it "Naturalization Interview"—which was designed to show I knew enough about making a living here and would not be a "burden" of some kind. Several weeks after I passed, a judge had me take an oath to make everything formal. There was a bunch of new citizens in the courtroom going through the same thing. We all hugged and shook hands with each other at the end.

Mary helped me on the exam—she was only too glad, with nothing going on at all. She got from the library two books suggested by the Immigration: *The USA Customs and Institutions: A Survey of American Culture and Traditions* and *American Literature: A Beginner's Anthology*. For two or three days in the office Mary worked with me on the first book. We reviewed all "exercises" at the end of each chapter. We did this over and over again, for about five times. At night I read the literature book. It was to help me with my "English proficiency," which, according to the package I'd received, was a "prerequisite" for a citizen of the United States. Mary wanted to help on this part, too, but I didn't let her.

The result of our cooperation, much to our mutual pride, was that I passed in flying colors. The immigration officer, Mr. Shugart, even stood up to shake my hand. "I hope all my applicants are as qualified as you," he said. He walked me to the door, which was several steps from his partitioned cubicle. In other cubicles other officers were on the phone, doing paperwork, or drinking coffee. I was the only "applicant" there. When I stepped out, an old lady in traditional Vietnamese dress accompanied by a pretty teenage girl came in and went up to Mr. Shugart.

"Mr. Farrell, are you Mr. Farrell?" they asked. Mr. Shugart didn't say yes or no. He turned and went back to his desk. "Are you Mr. Farrell?" they asked again, to another officer, and got *him* to talk.

Earlier, Mr. Shugart began his test with inquiries about my past, using those "Personal History" questions on the Immigration forms, questions that I'd known only too well. This didn't take long. Then he wanted me to assure him, "in my own words," that I had always paid the taxes, obeyed the laws, stayed away from the Communist Party, and so on. After that he looked up very officially at the space above my head and rapid-fired:

"What is the function of the judicial branch of the American government?"

"What is the purpose of a jury?"

"When a person is accused of a crime, what is he entitled to?"

These questions were all from the "exercises" part of the first book, so I was just as quick with the answers:

"To interpret laws."

"To decide the issues in trials."

"Trial by jury."

He then came back with more and more rounds. Still nothing I couldn't handle. After about ten minutes of what you'd call "intense questioning," he became more relaxed and sank low into his swivel chair. The blue-paneled cubicle was small but comfortable. When he leaned back, the chair squeaked loudly, but that didn't seem to be bothersome for the office. There was a heavy smell, a mixture of coffee, cigarettes, and old papers. He stopped to check his folder.

"Good . . . fine," he said, "now we only need to prove you have enough knowledge about English."

"Yes, sir." I said, waiting. He stayed silent. "Maybe . . . maybe you want me to discuss some works in American literature?" I asked, trying to round up in my memory as much as I could about *American Literature: A Beginner's Anthology*.

There was still no response from him. He checked into his folder again. "I can discuss a couple of poems, maybe," I said, and seeing that he was still unimpressed, I made a more specific, and daring offer: "Poems of Wallace Stevens. I can, maybe, talk about the meanings of several of his poems?" I did study and memorize a couple of Stevens' poems in the book. There was no better way, I had thought, to prove how I could really *understand* than by talking about American poetry, and to show how much I had improved since way back when I could barely talk in whole sentences. But the man did not take up my offer.

"I could write a couple of paragraphs for you now, about the poems . . . " I quickly followed up, but regretted it right away. The whole thing was becoming very risky.

"Well . . . " the man said.

"Yes?"

"Can you write something for me?" he asked, and handed me the sheet in his folder. It was a page of all the questions he'd asked me. There were checks, markings, and his written comments all over the place. At the bottom of the page was a blank line. He pointed at the line and said, "Can you write 'I love America' for me?"

"I love America?" I asked.

"I love America."

I did what he said, taking the time to make sure of my neat penmanship. He read my writing and put the paper back in the folder.

"Good," he said, smiling for the first time. "We now have everything we need." He nodded. That's when he stood up and congratulated me.

After I left the Federal Building, I decided to take a walk and kill some time. I looked out to the streets and saw a number of people who were now my "fellow citizens." The hot dog vendor. The men and women in nice business suits. The bus drivers. The construction workers with hard hats. People in T-shirts waiting for the bus. People burning tires in a distant vacant lot. I walked in the darkening downtown streets and began to recite a Wallace Stevens poem, one that I had originally planned for the immigration officer. Some of the passersby who heard me mumbling glanced at me. I felt somewhat empty and wondered why this was so with the day being such an important milestone in my life. Then I turned my thoughts to the office, and was thinking about how everything of the day would be the subject of my conversation with Mary for at least a few days, maybe weeks, to come, when suddenly, someone honked at me.

"Hey, what's going on?" a man stuck his head out of a pickup and yelled. "You stupid or something?" I looked and found myself in the middle of the street.

I quickly turned and headed back for my car. That night I wrote a long letter to my father.

13. A True China Lover

ONLY TWO YEARS AFTER Coldwell Electronics International was founded, its management was "realigned." Roger lost his job. Mr. Coldwell fired him during one of our "China Positions Review" meetings. Roger didn't see it coming. Neither did anyone else. Mr. Coldwell himself probably didn't know he would end up firing Roger. Mr. Coldwell doesn't think about this kind of thing. During that meeting Mr. Coldwell asked many questions as usual. When he heard me giving some of the answers, he started questioning what all I was doing in the company. Roger and Sam quickly filled him in. Then Mr. Coldwell said to Sam, "Sounds like Eric can do whatever Roger is supposed to do . . . " Afterwards he simply sat there quietly. Sam nodded and said nothing.

"I must say Eric is a good example of how a fine young man can develop into a business leader," Roger said quickly, "if we really work with him."

There was no response from Mr. Coldwell. Roger added: "In two short years, we have seen Eric transformed into an old China hand. I know I have put in extra effort to help. The result, well, the result is something we can all be proud of."

"Roger . . . eh, Roger, Sam, and Eric," Mr. Coldwell said,

"may I ask you to stay for further conversation?" Mr. Coldwell pushed his chair back and waited. Everyone else left immediately. Then Mr. Coldwell quickly said to Sam, "I only want one person in this job. I want Eric." Then he stood up and walked out.

After that, Sam, Roger, and I just looked at each other. I didn't know what to make of the whole situation, or even if I should try. Sam began drawing quick lines on his notepad, as if crossing out something. Roger remained calm and quiet. He seemed somehow amused. "Well," Sam finally said to Roger, "you heard what he wants." Sam kept his eyes down on the notepad.

"Yup," Roger said, "I guess I did. This China thing is well taken care of anyway." Roger smiled at me. "Mr. Coldwell wants me to move on to other things. I don't know . . . I don't know what he wants now. This guy is always ahead of me, always." Roger shook his head. "I guess I'll sit down with him tomorrow for my new project." He picked up his pen from the table and slowly put it back in his shirt pocket. "Eric, my boy," he said to me, "you want to go get a drink?"

After leaving Coldwell Electronics International, Inc., Roger worked as a Vice President of Sales for a small commodity brokerage firm; after that he was unemployed for a couple of months; after that he was an "Events Director" for the Chamber of Commerce in the small city where he lived; after that he went into consulting work, lecturing sometimes about doing business in China. His directorship at Coldwell Electronics International, Inc., was never taken away from him, neither was his right to own, eventually, seven percent of the company. But all that doesn't mean much now.

Roger's departure did not increase my workload much, since

he and I had been doing very much the same things, like Mr. Coldwell had said, and I had usually ended up doing most of them. But Roger had been sort of an authority on China for Mr. Coldwell, Carolyn, William, Sam, and, to a certain extent, for me. He was our official interpreter of Chinese philosophy, politics, laws, and social customs. More importantly, he was the one to articulate on why the people at China People's Electronics Import & Export Corporation, Madame Li and company, had consistently failed to perform. And all that, being a spokesman for the Chinese, was too tough a job for me. I did not have Roger's imaginative visions, much less his language skills. Roger had often described our frequent disasters in China with words sounding rational, less-threatening, and incidental. Words like "unintentional," "random," and "perceptual dissimilarity." I could only hope that nobody would bring up the "going-ons" in China.

After Roger had left, I went with Sam to as many meetings as I had to, but I spoke very little most of the time. That, however, did not seem to bother anybody. In addition, I still tended to my usual duties: translating Chinese reports and documents, writing letters and sending telexes to Madame Li and her people, calling them up on the phone—waking them in their sleep—when things got hairy, hosting delegation visits, and, when a real crisis hit, getting on a plane to go to Beijing.

As for the Chinese, I have yet to figure out why it was that, for them, business was so difficult. Or what exactly it was that made even a small buy, or sell, seem their impossible dream. You can't say they were not interested. That would be unfair. Compared to all of us at Coldwell Electronics International, Inc., they were only more dedicated to the work. Seven days a week. Twenty-four hours a day. At times we might say they were wasting time and energy, but never, in clear conscience, that they didn't put in the labor. And also, they always seemed so humble, so in need of help that no one, not us anyway, could possibly look away.

It had always seemed to me that the Chinese as a nation knew exactly where their gold mine was, and were prepared to give *generations* of lives for it. Westerners were more than welcome to join in the dig, for an eventual share of it. But the rocks were hard and the earth was thick, those who couldn't hang on for the long haul, those Westerners, would, one by one, fall away. So you saw many Westerners go in, with new products, new technology, new money, and so on, and just as many come out, completely exhausted and empty-handed. But the dig went on. And on. More Westerners would plunge in, until each of their resources dried up, and they, too, gave way to the next batch of newcomers. Not the Chinese. They didn't go in or out. They were, and will always be, there at the ready. Waiting for their day to come.

In March of 1981, the *Morning News* carried a long story about Mr. Coldwell and Coldwell Electronics International, Inc. It was written by Kathy Moore, a young journalist for the Business section of the *News*. Ms. Moore told her readers, in the story, that Mr. Coldwell, the insurance tycoon, had been given an exclusive right by the government of China to sell Chinese electronic products worldwide. According to Ms. Moore, Mr. Coldwell said the business in the next three to four years was to be "as much as sixty million dollars." And this would only be "the tip of the iceberg," because eventually, "low-cost, high-quality Chinese products will dominate the industry." Ms. Moore reminded her readers of the importance of her story by showing a diagram of how the Japanese "conquered the world of electronics." The diagram was entitled "Sales of Japanese Electronics 1970–1980." It showed a thick line that rose steeply and ended in an upward arrow outside the border of the diagram. "An arrangement of such magnitude," Ms. Moore wrote, "has never been made by the Chinese government before." At the end of the article, Ms. Moore summarized: "A true China lover is loved back by China."

The interview for the story was at Mr. Coldwell's fourteen-acre residence in the Riverpark area. Mr. Coldwell sat in his antique chair. Ms. Moore sat in a sofa with her legs nicely crossed. There was a piece of bright green Chinese jade sitting on top of a late Ching Dynasty low table in front of Ms. Moore. The living room was tall and spacious. You could see the garden landscape through the tall windows. It's a room intended for the visitors to behave in their more formal ways. Mr. Coldwell's niece and nephew, Carolyn and William, were also in the room. So was Sam. So was I. Sam and I had just returned from China and had been asked to "sit in support" of Mr. Coldwell.

"Getting back to this agreement," said Ms. Moore, close to the end of interview, "why do you think the Chinese chose to enter such a commitment with you? Why you? I mean there are certainly others . . . I mean, is there a special reason?" Ms. Moore was about twenty-eight or nine. She was attractive and her makeup was slightly visible.

"Oh, I don't know . . . You know, Kathy," Mr. Coldwell pointed at Ms. Moore, "the one most important thing is whether we can do a good job for them. I bet you if we work hard, and do not fail them, they're going to give us back ten, twenty times what we put in. I bet you.

"The Chinese are the most dependable people," Mr. Coldwell continued; "they are the most hard-working. You get these people started on something—watch out. They are going to make it. They are going to succeed."

"Is it accurate to say there is an even larger agreement between you and the Chinese leaders, and the electronics business is only part of it?" Ms. Moore asked.

"Well, I wouldn't think so . . . " Mr. Coldwell turned to Sam. "George . . . eh, Geor—"

"Sam," I said, softly.

"Yes, Sam," Mr. Coldwell said. "Sam here just returned from China. He is our president of the . . . the company. He's running this whole thing."

Ms. Moore looked at Sam and smiled. Sam pulled up his chair and said, "Well, I'll have to say there is a larger understanding, rather than a real agreement. It has a lot to do with a mutual feeling of trust. There are certainly others who might be able to take on such responsibility. But the Chinese may not trust them. Mr. Coldwell certainly is well respected . . . and trusted in China by the high-level leaders. That makes a relationship easier." Sam paused for Ms. Moore to finish writing. "You know, China is still in an infant stage of doing business with the West. They have to learn how to communicate with us, how to understand us, and so forth. Dealing with someone you trust is certainly the best way to begin."

"It might be we have a better standing in China than here," William said. He had taken off his coat earlier. His tie was loose.

"That's because the Chinese don't know us yet," said Carolyn. She laughed with everybody. The maid came in to refill everyone's drink. Ms. Moore put up her notepad and chatted with Carolyn for a while. Then she asked Sam some questions about the business before she left. She got the "sixty million dollars" part from Sam, not Mr. Coldwell.

After seeing Ms. Moore to the door, Sam asked Mr. Coldwell if it would be a good time to give him a briefing about our trip to China. Sam and I had just spent three weeks in Beijing.

"Shoot," Mr. Coldwell said.

"Well, we made good progress in getting a complete understanding about the manufacturing problems. The Chinese gave us very detailed reports at the factory level on their production process—"

"Are they going to be able to solve the problems?" Mr. Coldwell stopped Sam.

"They should. These are all technical problems. They seem to require a larger amount of information—"

"When do you think we can turn this around?"

"Well, we hope they will act very fast when they receive the technical data we are about to send them. I'd think by the end of the year we should be able to see some shipment from them. The schedule is—"

"What do we do until then?"

"We continue to seek other orders, we continue to prepare the Chinese for more production and shipments."

"You know, one of the worst things in business is surprises. We are not afraid of failures. If we know they are coming, we can handle them. But we don't like surprises. You can't run a business with a lot of surprises."

"No, sir," Sam said.

"Do the Chinese understand our objectives?"

"Yes."

"Do they appreciate our efforts?"

"Yes, sir. They sure do."

"Tell them not to worry about money. Money is there. We'll do a good job for them."

"Yes, sir."

"And we will succeed."

"Yes, sir."

On the way back to the office, I asked Sam if Mr. Coldwell was thinking about shutting us down.

"It's possible. It's his money," Sam said. "If he doesn't see returns for a while, he's gonna call the whole thing off. You can't blame him. It's his money." Sam was driving. It was a beautiful spring day.

"What do you think he is in this for? Making more money?" I asked.

"No. I don't think so. Not quite, anyway."

"What, then?"

"The kids. Carolyn and William. They are young, they've had it easy, and they are just plain inexperienced. They don't know much about real life. The old man is scared to death for them." Sam shook his head. "Yup, he's scared to death for them, the old man's no fool. This China thing, if it pans out, can give them a chance to start something from scratch. Like the old man did. Well, more or less."

"If you ask me, things are in good shape already. Carolyn and William don't look to me like they have much to worry about."

"They don't. But they have to deal with people. People who make money for them. People who keep money for them. And if you don't know how average people work, inside," Sam patted his chest, "you wouldn't know how to deal with them. All you have is more and more people who 'just work' here. That's all."

We turned into Armstrong Boulevard. The winding tree-lined streets of Riverpark were behind us. We saw shopping centers behind big, empty parking lots and car dealerships with colorful banners in bright sunlight.

"You think Mr. Coldwell is a nice person?" I asked. There was still a good twenty minutes' drive.

"Well . . . sorry, do you want to get a hamburger or go back to the office for lunch?"

"Go back. To the cafeteria."

"Okay. You were saying?"

"Yeah, I was just asking . . . I was just asking if you think Mr. Coldwell is a nice man." Sam slowed to let a red pickup get in the lane. A young woman in the pickup waved and smiled at us; her blond hair danced in the wind as she drove by.

"Of course he is a nice man. He is an extremely nice man. With great ability too. After all, he built his billion-dollar empire from nothing. You've got to have some talents to do that." Sam looked at me. "But that's not the point anymore. He has gotten so big and important for many people, you and I included, that he has to be a lot more than just 'nice.' He has to be a lot more . . . To people around him, he can be either the greatest or the most wicked. In a way, I would hate to be in his shoes. You can't be a real person too much."

"But give you a few billion you will try your best," I said.

"Give me a few *million* I will," Sam grinned.

Nobody could have been nicer than Mr. Coldwell—nobody else could possibly have afforded to be *that* nice—back when the

Chinese came to his ranch for a weekend before the first formal contract was signed. He gave the Chinese the royal treatment. The wine for the catered, coat-and-tie dinner alone was about three hundred dollars a bottle (and I reported the price to Madame Li). A group of country singers was hired for the big barbecue lunch. Mr. Coldwell himself took the Chinese delegation, eight of them, on a tour of the lake in a boat. All of us at Coldwell Electronics International, Inc., had a great time too. I helped the guests on the motorcycles and the three-wheeled bikes that you can go anywhere with. Mr. Yeh of the Planning Division got on a motorcycle, and it was soon after that he drove it into the lake. I saw his wild eyes and ear-to-ear grin when he was racing forward, and the next minute he was trying to crawl out of a pool of mud, his red motorcycle sinking in the water. He was terribly confused. And embarrassed. And wet.

It was apparent that the kind of fun we were letting the Chinese have was way over their heads. Most of them had never held a tennis racket in their lives, let alone having the tennis court, the sauna, the indoor pool, the skeet range, the lake, the pine forest, the horses, the motor boats, the canoes, and so on and so on all to themselves. The towels in their bathrooms were warmed at nights. And when they played pool, an electronic screen kept the scores.

But Mr. Coldwell kept asking me if the Chinese were enjoying themselves. I would be at the barn or by the lake or walking in the woods or somewhere, and he would spot me and come by.

"Hi, Eric," he would say, "is everything all right with the Chinese? Everything okay?"

A couple of times, he would put his arm around my shoulders and wait attentively for an answer. He looked unsure and very concerned. I wanted to say something like, "You've given them a ball, Mr. Coldwell. They don't even dream of stuff like this. Never in their life again will they have it so good either, if you ask me. Not ever."

Instead, I would say, as politely as I could, "Everything is going well, Mr. Coldwell."

Mr. Coldwell's niece, Carolyn, was also at the ranch for the Chinese. She pretty much kept to herself, though, spending most of the afternoon in the study watching a movie and reading office papers. When I was in and out of the house getting drinks and ice cream for the guests, I did manage to tell her how wonderful I thought the party was going.

"That's nice," she said to me as she put the papers down. "Good."

The only other time Carolyn Coldwell talked to me at the ranch was during the dinner. I was assigned to the table she hosted. The main guest for the table was Mr. Huang, the party functionary who had the title Manager of Components Manufacturing of China People's Electronics Import & Export Corporation. Carolyn explained to Mr. Huang how grateful she was that her husband had "taught her to stand up to her uncle." She told Mr. Huang that her husband, George, was the man who had told her she could have her own ideas. His advice had "changed her entire life." Mr. Huang, though fluent in English, had a difficult time trying to understand Carolyn's point. So I was asked, by Carolyn, to explain the whole thing in Chinese.

On the day he was fired, Roger gave me advice on doing business with China. He said, "I don't know what they are interested in, Eric. These Chinese. They are definitely not interested in business." Roger shrugged his shoulders and loosened his yellow silk tie. We were walking down to the cafeteria for a Coke. "I can tell you that now. But they sure are interested in getting you all excited about doing business with them." Then he poked his finger at my shoulder and said, "Always remember, don't get your hopes up. Never expect anything from them."

14. OUR DUSTER

AS OUR SECOND SEMESTER at Texas Tech drew to its final weeks, four of us, George, Tang-I, Frank, and me, still moved in a small tight pack. We still acted frequently in unison, faithfully following each other at the library, in the post office, crossing the campus, going to the grocery store, the bank, the barber shop, and so on, allowing only the differences in our class and part-time job schedules to temporarily divide us. Victor's rides, which had originally grouped us out of convenience, were now more good excuses to gather and chat.

"What's the program today?" we would ask each other at the breakfast table in the dorm. And whatever timetable we jointly worked out in the next few minutes we would loyally observe. Merely ten months ago we had been total strangers; now we wondered if we would ever again have better and closer friends.

The fact was we *relied on* each other. We needed these routine encounters to sort out new findings in our lives—those that were wrong, the misunderstandings, were potentially dangerous and we had to abandon them, in time, before they caused us serious damages. And this type of meeting was too important to admit new, untried members.

Then, on a night a few days before he left Lubbock, Victor turned over his car, a '69 Plymouth Duster, to our group.

"Don't ask for too much," Victor said as he put the car key in Tang-I's hand. "This car has seen its days. You can't get too much out of it anymore. It can be *unsafe* for you, I just want you all to know, if you don't handle it right." We had been slowly returning to Sneed Hall from the library when we saw Victor waiting for us under a tree. It was about eleven at night, a bright yellow moon was in the clear sky and cast moving shadows of tree leaves on Victor. "But take it anyway, and take good care of it."

"No, no, you don't have to do this, you don't have to do this . . . " Tang-I kept repeating. He shook his head and waved both hands earnestly, but he had a big smile on his face. All four of us were moved, and surprised, by Victor's generosity. Frank and I simply did not know what to say. George jumped up and down, opened his eyes and mouth wide, and said "Wow—" several times. It was kind of funny, to see him get into American-like facial and verbal expressions at a time like this. Then again, gratitude expressed in our humble Chinese ways might sound tame and insincere in Lubbock, Texas.

The Duster, blue with gold stripes, was parked illegally alongside the red curb, a few yards away from us. It was without even a small dent, and Victor had always kept it clean and shiny. We quickly moved over and walked around the car, our heartbeats quickening and our minds beginning to sense the coming, and exciting, change of life-style.

"It's still so new!" Tang-I said. "What do you mean—unsafe?" Tang-I kicked one of the tires nervously, probably unsure about his question.

"Mileage. You should always judge the condition of a car by its mileage. This car has over 78,000 miles—"

"And that's bad?" Tang-I interrupted.

"That's very bad. American cars are only good for 50,000 miles. After that you should buy a new one. That's the way with American society," Victor continued. He turned to Tang-I and gestured. "So, remember, mileage. Fifty thousand miles. And this car has a lot more than that." Victor kicked one of the tires, too, much harder than Tang-I did. "Learn to drive in it, and when you are through—when every one of you gets a driver's license, just sell it to a junkyard. It's not worth fixing it anymore."

"Of course we will take good care of it, of course," Frank said quickly. "Don't worry, we'll keep it well." He looked to the rest of us for support. We all nodded.

"And, we will learn to maintain it," George said. "When we leave Lubbock one day, we'll give it to other new students, just like what you are doing."

"Yeah, right, right," the rest of us said. The campus was very quiet, and whenever any of us said something, there was a faint echo.

Up till now, being in a car for a ride somewhere, anywhere, had been a privilege for us. We had each secretly toyed with the idea of working more hours and eventually buying a used car. But it was a remote concept, almost absurd, since none of the four of us knew how to drive yet. The Duster, quiet and still in the driveway that curved wide along the edge of Sneed Hall's immense Bermuda-grass lawn, looked ready to race through the campus, and then out on the streets, across the vast cotton fields, and further out to the east, where the land was dark, unmarked, and boundless.

"I only have time to teach one of you to drive," Victor said. "So the rest of you have to learn from him. Okay?" Right away we chose Tang-I, a Mechanical Engineering doctoral candidate, as the first trainee. Victor and Tang-I then took off in the Duster. We waited in the lobby of the dorm for about two hours, talking nonstop about what a great fellow Victor was and about how we should take care of *our* car.

Victor was to take a plane to Houston in the next few days. His company, Petrochem, had mailed him a set of air tickets which we had all seen with envy. The company had also planned to send a big truck for Victor to move his "furnishings and household goods," but since everything he owned could be packed in two suitcases (if he threw away nothing), the company wired two hundred dollars instead, to help with the "freight charges." Everything Victor's company had done for him had been an instant subject of serious discussions in the Chinese student community. They, the company's benefits, would be filed in our memories for reference, as yardsticks with which we would measure the courtesies provided us by our future employers, if and when we found ours.

One day a rumor had circulated that Petrochem was buying Victor an apartment in Houston. This had been quickly investigated, dismissed, and replaced with truth—there was to be "lodging assistance" through which Victor could get up to one month's rent allowance while he was looking for a place to live. Most of us had been so "nickel-and-dimed" to death by our unscrupulous employers at the part-time jobs that the treatment Victor was receiving sounded only too good. Victor let all of us read the correspondence he had received from Petrochem. And we had made copies of every page.

•   •   •

When Tang-I returned to the dorm from the driving lesson, it was almost two in the morning. George, Frank, and I had waited up for him in the lobby area of Sneed Hall. The three of us had been the only ones there since midnight. As Tang-I came through the door, we all rose from our seats. He looked a little tired but quite pleased. We could all see that he was trying hard to hide a wide grin. There was also a wild and proud appearance about him—the look of a returning hero. He walked toward us in big, brisk steps, and said, "I think I am getting the hang of it." He took a deep breath. "I only need a few days to practice, a few more days, then I will be ready to teach all of you."

"Good." I gave him a pat on the back. According to the agreement we had worked out while the three of us were waiting, I was to be the next driver.

"Let's take another look at the car," George suggested. So we all went outside to the car, feeling its still-warm hood, kicking the tires, and wiping the dust off the windshield and window glasses. Tang-I went back up to his room first; the rest of us sat in the car and chatted.

A few days went by. Then another few. Every morning at breakfast we waited for Tang-I to inform us that *that* would be the day he could put me in the driver's seat and start my first lesson. But he said nothing for a week. Afterwards we would begin to ask, gingerly, and he'd seem to deliberate long and seriously, then say hesitantly, "No, I need more time. I want to be absolutely sure about my ability to handle the car in all situations. It would be too irresponsible for me to teach you now." And that would be that. He wouldn't want to discuss it more, and whatever he didn't want we didn't do. He'd gotten all our respect, being the only one among us who could get in the Duster and take off. For *anywhere* he wanted. Each of the rest of us could be like him, too, but only sometime later, and with his help.

One afternoon Tang-I did invite the three of us for a short ride in a big parking area to the east of the Business School. He drove very slowly and demonstrated turns and parallel parking. The car kept leaning to the right of the road whenever he sped up; its tires scraped on the curb a couple of times. And when he tried to drive backward at about twenty miles per hour—a requirement of the driver's license test, he said—he almost collided with a stop sign. So we said to him, "Okay, you need to relax, take more time to practice, as much time as you need."

Back in the dorm the three of us decided to stop asking Tang-I for my driving lessons. And, as a show of support to him, we all contributed gas money. We also decided, with Tang-I's agreement, that we would share all future car repair bills in four equal ways.

A few more days passed, and Tang-I stopped talking about his driving practices altogether. We didn't ask either. Our group met as usual, and only in Tang-I's absences, which occurred more and more often, did the topics of cars or driving ever come up. One night, while Tang-I was out again with the car, we discussed the possibility that he might be permanently suffering from a poor sense of balance and that it could mean *months* before he learned to drive. Three weeks had passed since Victor had given us the Duster; two since he had left for Houston. I was still awaiting my turn at the steering wheel.

One afternoon I was hurrying from one class to the next, trying to run almost the entire length of the campus and at the same time catch my breath, when our beloved Duster swished by me. It dashed forward quietly, in sleek and graceful movement. Its blue color (wonderfully accented with gold stripes) blazed across my sight. The crossroad about twenty yards ahead made it slow down, but it regained power quickly, made a fine left turn, and continued speeding on. I could now see the driver, Tang-I, with his left elbow resting comfortably on top of the car door (the windows were down), and *only* his right hand on the steering wheel. His hair was blown slightly back by wind, as was the hair of his passenger, a girl in a red shirt—and I was almost sure it was Patricia Shiao, a good-looking new student from my country who had arrived a few days earlier.

For the rest of that afternoon in my classes I was too upset to concentrate. And as soon as I saw George and Frank at dinner, I gave them the terrible news. I described the Duster, the skillful driving (with one hand), the rolled-down windows, and *his* girl, Patricia Shiao. "Tang-I betrayed us," I concluded. At first George and Frank did not believe me. "It might be a different car that looked like our Duster," they said. Then they tried to rationalize Tang-I's disloyalty. With many different excuses. Then, one hour into the discussion, they were as mad as I was. And when Tang-I finally came back to the dorm at eleven-thirty that night (we were positive he had gone out on a date with Patricia *in our car*), we wasted no time giving him hell.

Tang-I did not expect to see the three of us so *infuriated*. But he kept his composure and calmly denied that he had done anything wrong. "I've not broken any promises, I am still practicing my driving every day. I am planning to teach you soon," he said, "in the next few days." There was not a trace of guilt in his voice.

The three of us yelled at him for a long time. He yelled back, too. In George's room, we went back and forth at each other and said many things that probably should not have been said. Then everyone was exhausted and fell quiet. The very loud music coming from the neighboring room began to bother us. Someone had probably turned on the stereo because of our fight. George pounded on the wall a few times. The music was turned up even louder. We then sat on the floor, listened to the music, and stared at the windows and the walls.

Finally, Tang-I got up. "Okay, if it'll make you guys happy. I'll teach Eric to drive today," he said. "Now. We can start now, if it'll make you all happy." Tang-I took out his car key. It was already past midnight, but we took him up on his offer anyway. Within minutes, I was behind the cool, smooth steering wheel of the Duster, waiting for the experience of my life.

"You are holding onto the steering wheel, as you know already," Tang-I said. He had made sure that I had my seat belt on first. "Steering wheel is what you use to control the direction of the car's movement.

"Then this is the brake," Tang-I continued. He didn't look at me in the eyes. He pointed and made sure I knew where the brake was by asking me to step on it a few times. "Gas pedal is right next to the brake. Be sure you do not confuse the two. Or it's big trouble," he said, still not looking at me.

"Okay," I said. "I won't confuse them. Don't worry." I began to think we had been a little too harsh on Tang-I.

"Next," Tang-I pointed ahead at the open parking lot, "you can turn on the ignition, and then shift the gear." He put my hand on the gear lever. "Shift the gear to D, then you are ready to go."

"Yes?" I waited for more step-by-step guidance.

"The rest is practice," Tang-I said. "So now you can start the car and begin to drive." Tang-I opened the car door on his side and stepped out.

"You mean I . . . I can drive now?" I asked.

"Yes, go ahead." He slammed the door shut, and talked to me from outside through the window.

"Wait . . . You are not coming along?" I asked.

"No."

"But how will I learn? How can I learn if you're not riding with me?"

"You'll just learn. This was how I learned from Victor in the first place. He never rode with me. I just practiced and practiced. That was how I learned. Really. You can do it too." Tang-I turned to walk away. He looked too serious to be joking.

"Wait a minute!" I yelled out to him. "Hey!" And he simply walked off. I forced myself to stay in the car, clutching onto the steering wheel with the tightest grips, talking loudly to myself to calm down, all the while thinking of going after Tang-I and punching him in the face.

That night I drove the Duster in a repeating square many times in the parking lot, keeping the speed less than twenty miles. I'd drive about twenty rounds, following the invisible lines of the square, making numerous right turns, then I'd reverse the direction to practice the left turns. I did this until dawn, never feeling sleepy throughout the night, and in early morning I was able to drive the car back to its usual parking space, about a mile away. At the breakfast table I declared to my group that I was ready to drive in the streets. Tang-I was with us, too. He still would not look at me, but I was no longer mad at him.

The next night George and Frank both insisted on getting their shares of time with the car. I taught both of them, using Tang-I's

140

(or Victor's) method. The three of us took turns driving in the campus parking areas for the next few nights. Then another fight broke out among us because Tang-I complained that he was no longer getting *his* time with the car, and because the other three of us all wanted to use the car in early evenings, when the shops were still open and the street traffics were busy enough to hone our driving skills. We quickly worked out a schedule. Afterwards we waited daily, in good patience, for our turn to take the Duster to wherever we wanted. The four of us did not meet regularly anymore, and when we did meet, occasionally, we talked about football games or grocery store sales or higher prices of postage or the new girl students from our country—things that didn't really matter, that we could say to *anybody*.

But nightly one of us would be with our Duster. We would each roam the streets of Lubbock, exploring our own favorite city corners, driving for hours and hours, all without a driver's license.

Soon the repair bills began to add up and our equally-shared gasoline charges became a hot subject of debate. Privately we blamed each other for overusing the Duster, and for the lack of proper car care, but we each rolled up the sleeves, from time to time, to change the oil, clean the carburetor, replace the water pump, and so on. We had some fun tinkering with the car and we learned words like "automatic transmission," "differential gears," "scheduled maintenance," and "a lemon."

Then came the summer vacation, and with our very different summer job plans, we sort of anticipated the inevitable, too —that we wouldn't be able to share the Duster much longer. One evening we talked in the library and Tang-I proposed a plan.

"I'll give you each one hundred for the Duster," he said. "You guys can use the money to buy a used car, if you want to." That sounded fair to us. The next day we would accept Tang-I's money, and in about two weeks each of us would have purchased a used car.

I would take my '64 Buick Le Sabre, at 89,631 miles, from Lubbock to Albany, New York, for a job as a lifeguard at the swimming pool of Tom Sawyer's Motor Inn. By the time I arrived in Albany, I would have replaced two shock absorbers (at the gas station attendants' insistence), fixed a flat tire, repaired a transmission oil leak, and, with all the money I had left, overhauled the engine. I would not drive my car for the rest of that summer. And when the time came for me to leave Albany, I would take a plane.

Tang-I would stay in Lubbock doing summer research for his professor. He would date often with Patricia Shiao. They would go everywhere in the Duster, even to her babysitting jobs. One night Patricia and Tang-I would give a little two-year-old boy a bath. They would mistake a can of Ajax for baby powder and sprinkle the harsh blue chemical all over the baby. The parents would be horrified when they found out. They would threaten to sue Tang-I, Patricia, and Texas Tech. The school then would cancel Tang-I's remaining summer contract and bar Patricia from any future part-time jobs to appease the parents. And Tang-I and Patricia would break up soon afterward.

George would be driving his '66 VW Beetle on the way to an Atlanta food company for the summer internship when he would get sleepy and fall off a highway ramp in Houston. There would be many stitches needed on his head, and he would lie in a hospital bed for about two weeks.

Frank would also get himself a VW Beetle. He would use it very little. His teaching assistantship would be extended for the summer. And he would stay in the dorm and drive his car only occasionally. Still, he would get two speeding tickets.

The four of us would not speak to each other for the whole summer, and most of the following fall semester. When we finally got together, it would be near Christmas, the finals would be completely over and we would have a lot of time at our hands and feel lonely. We would call each other up to suggest a "Christmas dinner party" at the Gridiron Steakhouse on Broadway and 7th Street.

The Gridiron was perfect for foreign students because of its "Red Raiders' Special"—a bargain-priced meal of salad, filet mignon steak, baked potato, desert, and iced tea or soft drink for $6.99. Complimentary and delicious blueberry muffins were also served several times at the table. We liked it because we knew exactly how much we'd be spending. And also we did not have to worry much about ordering. We only had to say, "Red Raiders' Special, medium," "thousand island," and "iced tea" to conclude the order. Everybody could handle that. And even if you forgot, you could say "same here," which was even easier.

Our "Christmas dinner party" was actually a big lunch because Red Raiders' Specials were only available during noon hours. We arrived in Tang-I's Duster at about one when the steakhouse was very crowded, but we were seated immediately. The party was a nice reunion for us, and although we didn't seem to feel the close friendship as before, it was still fun with everybody talking about their newer experiences, including the summer tragedies. We joked around a lot, talked on and on, very loudly, and never forgetting to accept the new batches of freshly baked blueberry muffins and iced tea refills. When the check came, Tang-I said, "Eight dollars and four cents each," and began to dig into his pocket. The rest of us quickly followed suit. Tang-I had added fifteen percent tip on top of six ninety-nine for everybody already.

"Here's eight-oh-four exactly." Tang-I threw a bunch of dollar bills and a few coins on the table.

"Here's mine," George said. "I'm four cents short. I only have dollar bills left."

"Me too," Frank also put his money on the table. "I'm four cents short too."

"I've got nine dollars here," I said. "That should cover everybody."

"No, no." Tang-I quickly threw a dollar bill back to me. "We only pay fifteen percent tip and not more. That's customary." He reached into his pocket again. "We need twelve cents more . . . and . . . here, I've got a nickel. We need seven more cents." He put the nickel on the table, making a sharp noise. "Look into your pockets. Hurry."

So everyone searched more. George stood up to reach deeper inside his pockets. "I don't have any coins!" he announced.

"Look more," Tang-I insisted. "I don't want to pay more than we have to. Everybody help!"

But none of us could come up with any more coins. We also ruled out paying one dollar more and getting back the seventy-eight-cent change. "The waitress wouldn't like that," Tang-I said. We must have spent over five minutes rummaging through our pockets for nothing. Then, a man in a gray three-piece suit came up to our table and stood behind George. With a hand, he tapped on George's shoulder. "Sir," he said. George turned around, surprised.

"How do you do. My name is Ron Mullen." The man smiled.

"Yes?" George said. We all looked at each other.

"I am an attorney here in town," the man continued. He was still smiling. His voice was soft and friendly. "You guys doing all right?"

"Yes," Frank replied. He stared at the man inquisitively. So did the rest of us.

"That's good," the man continued. "Is everything okay?"

"Yes."

"Well, good," the man said. "That's wonderful." He took a step back and gave a business card to George. "Now, if you have any problem at all with the bill, I am happy to take care of it."

"Problems? Bill?" George was getting more puzzled by the minute, as were the rest of us.

"Yes, if you are short in cash or something." The man lowered his voice somewhat. "I'm sure it happens to everyone. People sometimes just forget to bring enough money, you know." He took out his wallet. "I'll be more than happy to help."

"Oh, no, no, we're okay!" I said in a hurry. I tossed my dollar bill back on the table. "We have enough money . . . it's just that . . . " I glanced about at the others, hoping to get help with the explanation. But they all were just as embarrassed and tongue-tied.

"Fine. Just to let you know I'm glad to help." The man shook George's hand and walked back to his table. And without waiting for our change, we all rushed out of the restaurant. No one even thanked the nice gentleman once.

"Well, you live and you learn," Tang-I sighed as we were walking toward the parking lot.

"No. I don't think we'll ever learn." George said.

"Come on," I said, "this is an incident, a misunderstanding, that's all. You should be used to situations like this by now." I put my hand on George's shoulder. "Don't get *depressed* or anything."

"No, really." George turned to me, his glasses reflecting the bright sunlight. "I mean it. I don't think we'll ever really learn. As long as we are here. For the rest of our lives."

"Surely you'd agree that time can help . . . " Tang-I said.

"There will be other mistakes. Other embarrassment. People will still think we're strange ten years from now." George shook his head. "Or twenty. Thirty. As long as we're here. For the rest of our lives."

"Okay," I said. "Enough already." Somehow George's heavy words were hard to brush off. And as we moved away from the restaurant and into the sun, those cheery moments at dinner seemed to me distant and brief. "You want to take a long drive out of the city to see the sunset?" George said, changing the subject. We still had plenty of time to kill.

"It's too early," Frank pointed to the west. The sun was still bright—it was only a little after three. "Besides, you can see sunset from anywhere, every day. What's the big deal?"

The sight of a setting sun was a lot harder to come by in our island country. Our cities were congested with small buildings and surrounded with mountains, and our sky was always foggy from too much coal-burning. In Lubbock you could see the big sun and the wide open sky almost anywhere.

"I know a place you can see *good* sunset," George said.

"Where?" we all asked.

"I'll take you," George smiled mysteriously. He got into Tang-I's Duster. "Let's go!" He waved. We all got into the car, too. None of us had anything else to do.

The Duster still ran beautifully. In the car Tang-I bragged about its good gas mileage and how little he had to repair it anymore. George and I were looking for other used cars to buy at the time, and Frank still had his Beetle, which he still drove very little. The four of us had not traveled together since Victor had left us the Duster.

George directed Tang-I to go south and get on Loop 289, then east to catch state highway 84. We then went southeast on the highway for over an hour, leaving Lubbock well behind us. We went about fifty miles per hour and passed nothing but flat land. There were no trees or anything on either side of highway 84. Then, George said, "Okay, you can stop here." Tang-I pulled to the right and parked on the highway shoulder. There were no cars going or coming, and we were out in nowhere.

"Here?" Tang-I asked. Everyone but George quickly looked around.

"Yes," George said, matter-of-factly.

"But we are not in any *place*," Tang-I protested. "And what do you want us to see?"

"This a joke of yours?" Frank said, sticking his head out of the window. "No, no," George explained. "Just settle down. Look at the sunset." We turned to the right. "Isn't it great?" George continued. "The sun, the land, the sky. Nothing more. Pure sunset." George held out both his hands toward the sun.

Either Tang-I or Frank snickered. But then, doubtfully, we all looked again—George seemed very sincere. There was not a piece of cloud in the sky, no flocks of sparrows or other birds either, and not a single airplane above. The sky was clear, transparent-looking, for as far as you could see. It was a deeper blue way up on top, then turning a little grayish closer to the sun, then bright white. The sun was still quite a distance above the horizon—a small ring burning white. And the part of the sky below the sun was also white, and was met by a dark, straight line extending on forever horizontally. From that line the earth, dry and brown, stretched toward us and then way beyond. It was as wide as the sky, and just as uncluttered. Only a few trees could be seen in a very far corner. They were too small, and too invisible, to be considered adding to the land. All we had before us, like George had said, was the sky, the land, and the sun. There was not even the sound of wind. If you could have looked down from above in the sky, you could, of course, also have seen the very long, very straight highway, and in the middle of it, the tiny Duster with the four of us in it. Around us was one of those sceneries that you would not notice unless someone had pointed it out for you. For the four of us, who had come from a small island, it was a great sight. We all began to appreciate what George had meant by a *good* sunset, although none of us said a thing. We sat in silence and watched the sun lower, little by little, turning more and more orange, and beginning to sink into the land. It was, in fact, the first time we had a good look at anything in America. We let the time pass; then, when the sun was almost gone, we began to talk about our homes, our childhood, and our past friends. We began to talk in the way as if we were back in the earlier days when Victor was still around. There were again the feelings of closeness and camaraderie. And in the middle of it all—the majestic scene, the hearty talk—every one of us suddenly became homesick. We continued to talk, but one by one, I knew, we all felt terrible inside. We had not missed home that much—we had had no time for that. The sunset gave us the time. And the place.

•   •   •

Later that evening we would talk less and less. And when it was dark, Tang-I started the car engine.

"You know where we'd end up," George suddenly asked, "if we kept going forward on this highway?"

"Dellas," Tang-I replied.

"Yeah," George agreed.

"Let's go back," I said. And Tang-I turned his car around.

Tang-I sped up to almost ninety-five miles per hour on the way back. We would be back in Lubbock in less than thirty minutes. We would say simple goodbyes to each other and, after that evening, would not have an occasion to meet as a group again.

15. Fish in Ponds

ONE DAY AT LUNCH, Sam said to me if we were all to get fired, it would be because of Carolyn Coldwell. We were only at the end of the second year then. Roger had just been fired, and I'd become Special Advisor reporting to Sam. To me, Sam sounded a little drastic about it all. There had always been rumors in different shapes and forms, since Day One, about how we wouldn't last six more months and all that.

"Why, you know something we don't?" I said, trying to be casual.

"Oh . . . I don't know. You never know what's going to happen anymore. Everything's so tentative," Sam said. We'd had a string of bad news from China; everyone was frustrated.

"And you think they'll fire us soon," I said.

"Well, it's not out of the question. It's their money, you know." Sam stared at me. His eyes looked tired. He had been working in his spare time to help his wife start a small beauty shop.

"Well, I guess there are other places to go, if it comes down to that," I said, still trying to be casual.

"Yes. You and I can go back to Taltex."

"Yeah."

"But it's like this." Sam was getting more interested in the conversation. He took out a pen and quickly drew on a paper napkin. "You and I are like fish in the pond." Sam drew three or four fish with a big circle around them. "Now, the water is getting lower, it's getting harder to breath." Sam pointed to the fish he'd drawn. "It's getting worse and worse because the water is getting lower and lower. And you say to the fish, there are other ponds. Of course there are. Maybe much bigger and better ones, maybe a lot of them." Sam raised his eyes to look into mine. "But it won't do the fish any good unless they have a way to get there. Right?" He slammed his hand down on the napkin, covering the fish pond entirely.

"No, I guess not." I didn't want to get him going again. Sam could be very intense if you got him started. "So, what does it have to do with Carolyn Coldwell, for God's sake?" I asked. "Other than the fact the old man's money is also hers, and we could be spending hers."

"That's good enough reason for me, pal," Sam said, and lost interest in the conversation. He was occupied with his own thoughts for a while. Then we got up and left. Like I said, he could make you feel bad if he wanted to.

Being fired was something I never had to worry about when I worked at Taltex as a Systems Programmer/Analyst One. First of all, it was a big company, and there were all kinds of rules about firing people. That didn't mean you wouldn't get fired, you would, but you kind of knew, too, when and if it was coming. And supposedly you could be "corrective" about it, and change into a new person before they gave you the ax. Secondly, I never had any complaints from my bosses. They gave me programs to write, and

I'd go to my little corner with my own computer and write them for days, or weeks. My bosses wouldn't bother me and I wouldn't bother them. And thirdly, I must say I was a darn good computer programmer, for whatever it's worth. Once I was through with my stuff, they, those programs I wrote, would be so long and so complicated, only I could figure them out. And my bosses understood it perfectly; they themselves had once been so good they could not have been fired.

It was a very different story, though, when I was with this small farm equipment parts wholesale company in Lubbock. They started me as a night-shift computer operator, minimum wage. My job was to make sure the computer ran without a problem between four in the afternoon and midnight, six days a week. The way you could tell if there were problems was by listening. The computer beeped loudly when there was a reason, splashed words on the screen, and stopped, more or less, until the operator, I, did the right thing. I found the solutions by looking into the two thick operations manuals and a notebook left by a man who'd had the job before me. The man was Andy Thomas. He was now Operations Manager, my boss. My job was a lot more work than I had expected, and a lot less in pay. But at the time I'd just graduated from Texas Tech, and after having been rejected by about four hundred companies, it was the best I could hope for. I was beginning to like the quiet life in West Texas anyway.

A man by the name of Bob Whitman started this company during World War II and had made some money from it. Most of the people there had known and worked for Bob Whitman most of their adult life. It was kind of like a big family and all that. Nobody was getting rich or anything, except maybe Bob Whitman, but everybody had a job. In the office, people were as serious about the weather and football as they were about business.

When I started with the company, old man Whitman's two sons, Richard and Russell—Rick and Russ, as they were called —had taken over. Rick had the Accounting, the Marketing, and the warehouse. All Russ had was Data Processing, which was basically the computer, which I took care of between four P.M. and twelve A.M. Rick and Russ had problems with many people in the company who were much older than they and who had been like brothers to their dad. Rick and Russ also had problems, a great many, between themselves. There often were open quarrels between the brothers in the office. The situation was worsened when Russ's wife, Margie, and Rick's wife, Cindy, also came to work. It appeared to me, and others, that Rick was getting the best of Russ. I had seen Russ and Margie storming out of the office, vowing never to return, at least a few times. And I worked only the night shift then.

Anyway, after a couple of months and a million rounds with the beeping computer, I finally got pretty good at it. I was able to get everything in order by eight or nine, and had three or four hours to do almost nothing. Usually, I'd sit there and let the computer, now quiet and nice, bore me to death. Once in a while, I'd wander around in the warehouse, but it was very dark so I soon stopped.

One night a noise from the telephone room got me very nervous. The telephone room was next to the computer room. That's where our telephone operator worked during office hours. No one had a reason to be there in the night. No one was supposed to be in the company at all, but me, until midnight, when the security people would show up. So I sneaked around and went in the telephone room to see what was going on. A man was sitting by the switchboard and talking on the phone in a very low voice. I got closer, the man turned and saw me. It was Russ Whitman. He was as surprised as I. I was also frightened. I had no business sneaking up to Russ Whitman.

"I . . . I . . . I am so sorry," I muttered frantically.

Russ sighed. He had a small book in his hand. He looked at me with his glazed eyes as if trying to figure out what to do. I wanted to say I had heard or seen nothing, in case he had been talking company secrets or whatever. I wished he'd go back to whatever he was doing. I'd just go away. I didn't need any trouble.

"I . . . didn't know," I said. "I'm sorry."

Russ began to recover. He waved his book at me and said, "Well, since you are here, why don't you sit down." His voice was coarse and weak. "Maybe you can help me do this," he smiled awkwardly.

"Yes, uh, yes . . . "

"You can see I am making phone calls. And this is what you can do for me . . . "

Russ explained he was calling every number in that book. If there was no answer, he wanted me to mark N by the number. If there was someone there, he would either tell me to mark C or T. That was all I had to do.

The fact was, I had caught Russ in the most embarrassing moment of his life. Russ Whitman was calling every female student in the dormitories of Texas Tech University. He was making obscene phone calls. If the girl talked to him, even for a second, he would mark T on that number. If he was hung up on, it would be a C (for click). N was for no answer. Russ would call and mark every number on a page. He would call the N and T numbers back again and again, until all the numbers were Cs. Then he would do the next page. The book he held in his hand, with the covers torn off, was the student telephone directory, which I had known well. Russ thought I had figured out what had been going on when I went into the telephone room. I should have told him otherwise.

For the next three or four weeks, I helped Russ mark those numbers and handed him the numbers he could "still use." Every day. And every day I was worried to death that he was going to fire me. It was very tough on me. I couldn't figure out, and still can't, why Russ did what he did. Almost all the numbers were Cs at the first try. Russ was nervous and tense when he dialed the numbers. I did speed things up for him. When Russ got someone on the line who would talk, he would turn to the switchboard, lower his head, and speak in such a diminished voice it sounded as if he was praying. I felt sorry for him. And I felt a great deal of his loneliness, too.

Later, I was unexpectedly transferred to the day shift. And because of that, I stopped doing the telephone thing for Russ. I was still scared about losing my job, though. I read the classified job-section every day and sent out some resumés, only to have more rejections. A few months later, as I was getting close to landing a job at Taltex in Dallas, Andy, my boss, told me Russ and Margie had moved to Colorado to "start a new business."

"Off we go, to a whole new world," Andy sang to me as we were finishing up our chat. I looked at him curiously. Andy explained those were the words to a song he had heard.

"Off we go, to a whole new world," Andy sang again as he walked away.

16. BLACK FRIDAY

ON A SUMMER DAY OF 1984, I was told some bad news. I was told Victor had committed suicide in his own swimming pool in Houston six months before. I was told he had been laid off and had stayed home for a couple of months. His wife had been working full time then. She and their three children had been very shocked and saddened.

The person who told me this was Tom (formerly Tang-I). Neither Tom nor I expected we would see each other again, many years after Lubbock, at the drive-through Chinese food place on Coit and Campbell called Eggroll Express. Tom had owned that unit of the Eggroll Express franchise since late 1983 and had been running it himself.

I had been buying from Eggroll Express regularly for quite a while. Two or three times a week, I'd get Beef Broccoli or Kung-Pao Chicken with a lot of rice and wash it down in my apartment with Cokes. The food was only tolerable. The service was very fast. But on the day I saw Tom, the place was swamped with cars, and anyone who ordered other than eggrolls or chow mein had to wait for their orders in the small parking area. When Tom brought me the Beef Broccoli, I thought he looked very familiar, but didn't think too much of it until I was almost back in my apartment.

When I went back to Eggroll Express, Tom was still making deliveries in the parking area. He called me by my name as I stepped out of my car. "Let's go inside and talk," Tom said and he took off his green apron. I took my Beef Broccoli with me. Inside there were only four or five tables, bright orange and yellow, with black stools fastened to the floor. He got himself some Dr. Pepper in a large, red plastic cup almost full of ice.

"Nice. Are you the owner?" I asked.

"Only a small place." He stirred his drink with a straw. "Tough to make a living nowadays. How about you? I heard you are not doing too bad."

"Well, I've been working for this guy by the name of Coldwell. He is very wealthy. I've been traveling a lot to the Orient for him."

"That sounds very exciting. In this business, it's eighteen hours a day every day. Every day." Tom turned to yell instructions at the young man who was filling orders from behind a big counter. "You have to do everything yourself."

"But the money you make is all yours, unlike the situation I am in—"

"Tough business. It's tough to make any money nowadays. But you can't stop."

"I thought by now you'd be a full professor in some famous university . . . " I said, half jokingly. Tom had told us many times in Lubbock all he'd wanted was to be a professor.

"I was, until last fall. UT-El Paso." Tom looked absent-minded. "But I had to make a change. Now I have this."

"Is this better?"

"Yes and no. Well . . . I don't know. You tell me what is the best and I'll do it. Whatever is the best. I don't know what is the best . . . " Tom looked at me as if I was giving him a hard time. I changed the subject and talked about new buildings in the city and other nonsense. His customers kept coming, but he stayed with me. Occasionally he had to get tough with his people and yell his lungs out. Each time his place got busier, I could feel his spirit go up inside him, though he tried to keep calm about it.

Tom told me Victor had drowned himself in the pool, dressed in a tie and suit. They had found his briefcase at the bottom, opened, with papers scattering about in the water. His pair of Mont Blanc pens and his Rolex watch, too, at the bottom. When his wife returned home, she thought someone had thrown a pile of laundry into the pool. She sent the kids out to check. She told Tom everything had been normal and all that. Victor couldn't believe they'd lay him off, because he had always done well in the company, at least that's what he'd always believed, for eleven years. But his wife thought he would get over it. After all, it was a company-wide layoff, and Victor was one among two thousand.

"It was a layoff because of bad business conditions," Tom said. "Can't believe Victor got personal about it. He got too serious. Now what are his wife and three children to do? Did he think about that? Stupid, you know. That stupid man! You should at least think about your children!"

Tom and I couldn't talk much afterwards. His workers kept creating problems for him, and he was really giving them hell before I was even out of the door. I began driving for nowhere. I got on the highway and looped around the city for a good two hours. I felt so lousy I didn't want to be by myself in the apartment. I drove until I had to gas up. Then I went into the city library a block away from the gas station.

For no good reasons at all, I began to search the old newspaper files for the ones dated about a couple of months before the time of Victor's death. What I did was quite senseless, now that I look back. At the time it was the only thing I thought to do, though. I had to read the news about the layoff, or what Victor's company had said about the layoff.

It was not as easy as you might think, to go over three or four months' worth of newspapers. First of all, that was a bunch of newspapers. Secondly, there was a bunch of layoffs. Business was not good, for anybody. I was there for the rest of that night and the next two evenings before I finally found something in the *Morning News*. It was a tiny article compared to the other stories, only four short paragraphs, and it appeared in the last page of the Business section. Petrochem Announces Layoff was the title. Three words. Here are the first and second paragraphs:

PETROCHEM ANNOUNCES LAYOFFS

By Cynthia Jones
Staff Writer of The News

Petrochem today announced its plan to reduce its U.S. work force by two thousand.

A company spokesman cited business reasons for the layoff, Petrochem's first since 1981.

The third and fourth paragraphs were much longer. They talked about how the "second quarter earnings" were considerably less than that of the previous two years. And about which part of the company business was responsible for the "shortfalls" in "financial performances." They went on to say how the new "diversification initiatives" were supposed to lead the company to a much brighter picture, "according to Jeff Lambert, the Chairman."

I made a copy of the article, and kept it in my office. I felt a little of what Tom had said about Victor having been stupid. This thing about "business reasons" was just that, "business reasons." Nobody needed to die because of it. Nobody. Certainly not Victor.

In October of 1986, about three years after Petrochem had laid off Victor, I told twelve people they were no longer to come to work at Coldwell Electronics International, Inc. —also because of business reasons. I talked to these twelve people one by one. I told them the same thing. There was no reason to change my speech. It worked equally well for every one of the twelve. By five o'clock that afternoon, October 14, 1986, the Black Friday, all these twelve people were gone from the office of Coldwell Electronics International, Inc. I have not seen any of them since. Here is what I told each of the twelve people:

"(Name), I am afraid I have bad news for you. Mr. Coldwell has decided not to support a number of our programs. And (name), I am very sorry, but we must ask you to leave. This is strictly business, you understand, (name). We have no complaint about your performances. On the contrary, we are impressed with your dedication and professionalism. We have been struggling to make this work, and you've done more than your share. But we simply did not succeed. If there's anybody to blame at all, it's probably the management, I included. We didn't foresee the pitfalls that led the company to one problem after another. Anyway, the bottom line is Mr. Coldwell wants to cut people right away.

You'll have two weeks' severance in addition to your earned vacation pay. A check is ready for you at the personnel department. I hope this will not be too difficult for you, (name). I want to say again, it's not your performances.

If you need a reference or anything, please let me know. And we'd be happy to forward all your messages."

The Black Friday at Coldwell Electronics International, Inc. I'll tell you more about it later. For now, I only want you to know what I've told you.

The point is, people are generally nice about it, if you know what I mean. You can dump a lot on people with this business stuff. If they live to be ugly about it afterwards, heaven forbids, you can pretty much shut them up, too. That's about the size of it. Suppose I had gone bananas and gone all the way to the Chairman of Petrochem, this Lambert guy, and begun "demanding an explanation" like a lunatic. I'd still be getting what the newspaper had said already. If I got anything at all. Business reasons. No more and no less. And, if the other one thousand nine hundred and ninety-nine poor souls could have taken it "fairly well," what was the matter with Victor anyway?

What's to happen to me, possibly Mary too, is going to be the same thing. We'll be gone soon, the last two at Coldwell Electronics International, Inc. —for business reasons.

Mr. Coldwell used to have a secretary, Barbara, a few years back. She was well liked and, in my opinion, very attractive. She never acted like she was some hot shot just because she sat close to Mr. Coldwell. The others usually did, and they gave you such hard times for no good reasons. Barbara was becoming more important in the office with her receiving many guests on behalf of Mr. Coldwell and all that. We all had gotten quite used to her being there, taking care of things.

One day, she resigned and left. We couldn't believe it. None of the other secretaries would tell us why, not that they had ever talked. Months passed, and we, a small group at Coldwell Electronics International, Inc., who were not busy at the time, got a little sentimental. So we got together and asked Barbara, still unemployed, to lunch. We chose a Mexican restaurant which, I thought, had put in too many plants, and the food was plain second-class. We chose it because Jesse insisted it was the kind of Californian Mexican place he "just knew" Barbara would like. Anyway, I was looking forward to it. Partly because I liked the idea of seeing her again, and partly because I had always been curious, like others, about why she had left so suddenly.

Once I was kept waiting in the lobby outside of Mr. Coldwell's office for hours. Mr. Coldwell had called for me early in the morning; I'd hurried over immediately, and had been asked to stay in the lobby for the longest time waiting for a "break" in his schedule. After two hours, I began to wander about in the hallways, for no real purpose. I was in a quiet corner staring at an old painting of three Chinese monks under a pine tree. It was one of those antique paintings, I'd been told, that Mr. Coldwell had bought either in London or Hong Kong. I'd enjoyed it a great deal every time I'd been kept waiting. Then I heard someone rushing by me. I turned around and saw Barbara, almost running, heading for the ladies' room. I only saw the backside of her when I turned. Before she could get to the ladies' room, she stopped and put both her hands on her face. I could see from the way her shoulders moved she was weeping, although I could hear nothing. She quickly steadied herself and went into the ladies' room. I stood there, alone, not knowing what to make of it. I began pacing up and down the hallway over and over. Barbara had always been pleasant and businesslike and all that. I'd never seen her upset or anything. Knowing the number of jerks she had to deal with in that office, you'd think she'd have at least one major blowup a day. The other two secretaries—both had been with Mr. Coldwell for years—would snap at you before you had time to say hello. That's why Barbara was so popular. She never got nasty.

In about ten minutes, the ladies' room door pushed open and out came Barbara. I was then walking toward her. She had on the kind of sharp business outfit that you see on women executives. Her shirt, soft white, looked nice and fluffy on her. As she walked, bright light bounced off her shoulders, giving her face a tender and peaceful look. When she saw me, she smiled widely as usual.

"Hi, Eric," she greeted me.

"Oh, hi, Barbara, uh . . . " I did not know what I should say. I saw her smooth chin and white teeth when she came closer. And her very red eyes.

"You take care," she said, and turned into the side entrance of Mr. Coldwell's office. Her voice rang in my ears, and I thought I saw her wink at me.

It was almost another thirty minutes before Mr. Coldwell could see me. I saw Barbara again as I passed her to get to Mr. Coldwell's conference room. She was speaking with another secretary. Her hands were busy with a stack of papers. She looked as chipper and unruffled as she'd ever been. She saw me and said, "Mr. Coldwell's now expecting you, Eric." When she smiled, her eyes were as beautiful as always.

What Mr. Coldwell had wanted to talk to me about was only

some minor things. It took about three minutes. I passed at least four or five men in suits and shiny shoes waiting to see him when I left.

Our table for six at the Mexican restaurant was obviously too small. There were three plants around us. Every time you turned your head, you got some tree branches in the face. The good thing was we sat close to each other, with Barbara right in the middle. Jerry and Oliver, the two young engineers of the company, were seated at two sides of Barbara. Jesse, Sam, and I were across from her. Barbara looked relaxed and, in a way, happy. She joked with us and got into some serious discussions about how a dental operation had almost taken the life of her uncle in Houston. She said she wanted to take it easy for a couple more months, before getting back to a job. She had gotten several offers, she said, and Mr. Coldwell's reference had helped a lot. It was very easy for each of us to talk to her about whatever came to mind, like being with a lifelong friend. At least that's how I felt. If nothing else, it was a very delightful chat.

After a while, Sam asked, "Oh, by the way, how did you come to decide to leave? What made you quit Coldwell?"

"Yeah, you dropped us a bombshell. What happened?" Jerry said. He moved his chair forward so he could see more than just one side of Barbara's face.

Barbara gazed at the couple sitting a table away from us. With both hands, she moved her glass of iced tea closer. She smiled lightly and did not speak for some time. Then she leaned to her left to look at Sam and me. Her crisp white collar pressed against her long neck. "Oh, nothing really," she glanced around at all of us, "just business reasons."

"All right, uh . . . " Sam said. He mixed his salad quickly with a fork and didn't finish what he was saying.

Neither I nor anyone else said anything more for a while. Later, we kind of went on as if we'd never wanted to ask. There were more small talks. Sam picked up the dental stuff and lambasted doctors in general. Jerry and Oliver argued how the Chinese had been dishonest about one of the contracts we were negotiating. Jesse and I were mostly silent afterwards. So was Barbara.

The way I felt about it, the lunch gave all of us the time, finally, to say goodbye to Barbara. Barbara was as beautiful as she would always be in our memories. We knew too, most likely, we would not see her anymore. Life went on.

Well, not in Victor's case. That was different.

17. AS PRESIDENT

THE STORY OF Coldwell Electronics International, Inc., could not be simpler: Mr. Coldwell's money established it; for six years, Mr. Coldwell's money supported it; then one day Mr. Coldwell said enough's enough; he pulled the plug; the end.

There were, certainly, long reports at the end with thousands of tiny numbers which kind of told Mr. Coldwell, and anybody else who wanted to know, that if Mr. Coldwell didn't "terminate" the "project," meaning Coldwell Electronics International, Inc., he'd be so stupid that people would begin to laugh at him. The Senior Advisors and Analysts who did the reports were, by all means, reliable and had nothing but Mr. Coldwell's "best interests" in mind. They, these Senior Advisors and Analysts, also had done the long reports six years before, saying, more or less, that if Mr. Coldwell could not see his way clear to "become involved" in the "type of business" Coldwell Electronics International, Inc., set out to "originate," he would be passing up a "never-again opportunity."

Things had changed with time, of course.

What the thousands of tiny numbers said, in every possible way and more, was that the Coldwell Electronic International, Inc., people, meaning us, were a group of morons. That after Mr. Coldwell's "unremitting support," for an "extensive length of time," the employees at the Coldwell Electronics International, meaning us, had failed to "put the business on the course."

All this, I have to admit, was quite close to the facts, except, of course, for the moron part.

October 14, 1986, was a Tuesday. I have called it the Black Friday all along because it sounded right. I might have had other reasons, I don't remember and it's not important. For Dallas it was a day the "morning cloudiness" turned "hot and sunny" in the afternoon, and a fifteen-to-twenty mile per hour "southerly wind" blew all night long. It was also a day most of the nation suffered "rain showers and thunderstorms." And on this day in 1900, a lowest-ever temperature of forty-five was recorded.

The *Morning News* did not say a thing about the firing of twenty people at Coldwell Electronics International, Inc. The *News* reported many stories that day, using up fifty-three pages. There was a story about a professor in California who, after two and a half years of study, announced his findings on the "patterns of human clapping." Using scientific instrumentations and graduate students as "monitors," the professor had recorded "the frequency, loudness, and methods" of clapping by humans of "both sexes" and "different socio-economic strata." It was a long story broken into four parts, each printed on a different page. The two most interesting results of the research, said the *News*, was that men generally did not clap louder than women, and that "methods of clapping" had a lot to do with "levels of education."

There was also a story in the Metropolitan section about a 32-year-old woman, Vicki Newman. She was "petite, driven, a chain smoker and a nonstop gabber." And she wanted, the *News* said, to be the richest woman in the USA. She wanted to "earn it, not inherit it." She was a stock broker. In the Business section, a "management consultant," Jan Green, gave advice to "new managers" in her weekly column. One reader asked, "What should a new manager accomplish during the first two months on the job?" Jan Green replied:

> Establish yourself as a competent person who can keep
> things rolling, and get to know what your boss prefers. Does
> she like to look over your shoulders or be kept up-to-date a
> few times a week? Does he prefer verbal reports to written
> reports? If you don't have your boss's support, everything you
> do is going to be ten times more difficult.

I liked the "and get to know what your boss prefers" part. I thought it was hilarious. I also liked the big story the *News* was doing about Taltex. Only the second part was printed on October 14, 1986, because the story was very long. Supposedly it was going to take three more days to finish the whole thing. It, the second part, was basically on how Taltex was "expanding its international presence." It talked about how some of the management people at Taltex were going around the world making sure their factories "followed local customs." In Japan they had climbed to a Shinto shrine on top of Mount Tsukuba to pray for success for a new production line. And in France, they'd made rules to allow workers a glass of wine during lunches in the company's cafeteria and all that. The headline for this part of the story was TALTEX'S MELTING POT. Right under the headline it said, "Company policy, local customs mix at plants worldwide." I liked what the President of Taltex said in the story. "It's always easy to assume that because that's the way it is here in the United States, that's the way it's going to be in this country or that country," he said. "That's really not true. It's particularly important to take a little time to be sensitive to cultural differences around the world." I liked a great deal about "That's really not true." The story was full of other great stuff the President had said. You got suspicious now and then that the President himself might have written it.

Then, there was a very small article about a Korean man who had five wives, and all of them worked in his grocery store.

Anyway, nothing at all about the firings at Coldwell Electronics International, Inc., on that day or any other day. I'd like to make it clear in case someone gets carried away, like I did on Victor's company, and wants to know what *my* company had said in the paper. Nothing. Not that any decent newspaper would be interested.

In many ways, you couldn't get too excited about what happened on the Black Friday. For one thing, it was not the first time Coldwell Electronics International, Inc., had fired anybody. At least six or seven others had been fired before. Not all on the same day, of course, but still. There was a secretary, Kim, who got caught keeping a bottle of scotch in her drawer and drinking from it at times. The security people working for Mr. Coldwell said she was an alcoholic and had bought drugs on company property. So Sam and I fired her. Simple as that. I remember Kim bit her lip as Sam told her the news. She had on a white oversized sweater and a tight skirt that was kind of sexy. When Sam was through, we thought she was going to leave in tears or whatever and not to be heard from again. But she was quiet for only a second, then stared back at us with her cold eyes.

"But I haven't done anything wrong," she protested.

"You've been found to keep alcohol and drugs in the office, Kim, and that's against the rules. You know that, Kim," Sam explained slowly, trying to be friendly.

"You can't tell me what to do with my life."

"But, Kim . . . "

"Have I been late for work? Have I messed up anything? Have I left early? Tell me what I have done wrong." Kim's eyes grew bigger. She stared at Sam and me. She was very steady and calm. And she was fierce.

"No, Kim. We are not saying you've done anything wrong—in business. We are saying you violated the company rules by what you have done." Sam was a little edgy. He leaned back on his chair and swung his leg slightly.

"But I have not done anything wrong! Don't you get it? Business is business and my life is my life. As long as I don't mess up, what I do is my own business. You've got it wrong, not me. You can't fire me for what's going on in my life. You can't do that!" We were in the conference room with the door closed. The three of us sat around a big table. Kim rapped the table with her fist. Her other hand grabbed the top of the empty chair next to her. Sam looked at an ashtray in front of him.

"Well, Kim, I'm sorry. That's not how we think," Sam said, softly.

"Well, I think this is a bunch of bullshit! This is unfair! I'll talk to my lawyer about it," Kim threatened. Her head was held high, but the harshness was gone from her eyes. She stroked her sweater with one hand and went into a long silence. It was a frustrating kind of silence for the three of us. Awkward too. And a little embarrassing.

Finally, I said to Kim, "Maybe you'll have better luck with your next employer."

Kim bowed her head and sighed. Then she stood up and looked down on Sam and me. "Well, I'd hope so. God, I'd hope so." She quickly turned and left. All we heard afterwards was she went away to Oregon with her boyfriend. That Kim, she was one tough lady.

Then there was David Morley, the Financial Manager. I was involved in firing him, too. It was more of a cut-and-dry case because he was not doing anything right at all. I mean you could tell him to go down the hall and he could mess that up. There was something happening in his family that was so screwy that he simply couldn't concentrate. You saw him with a blank look all the time and you'd feel sorry for him and all that, but there was very little anyone could do to help. He wouldn't talk about it either. We kind of went along with him for a while until one day he made a big mistake with the books. It became obvious, even to him, that he couldn't hang on anymore. We told him to take a couple of months off to sort out his life. We would talk in two or three months, we told him, and see where we'd go from there. What we were really saying was, of course, he was no longer wanted. He knew it too. And the look on his face was a little scary. Like someone had shot him in the head. It took him a few minutes just to stand up. I remember shaking his cold, sweaty hand. I remember his unfocused eyes. Sam and I both got depressed for the longest time afterwards. It was as *unpleasant* as it could be. I mean really.

Most of us at Coldwell Electronics International, Inc., had never been fired before in our lives. Then again, nothing special there either. A lot of people in companies everywhere have never been fired, period. Just a fact of life. Granted, people may not always come out and tell you they have been fired, even if they have. This is the kind of thing you hear a lot about, and feel happening all around you, but, in reality, doesn't happen to everybody. I have never been fired. And I do not say it with a great pride. I have resigned several times, though. And believe me, there is a difference.

Sam had never been fired either. Taltex was the only place he had ever worked, for fifteen years, before he came to start Coldwell Electronics International, Inc. When he resigned at Taltex, he went directly to the Vice President in charge of the Defense Electronics Division, three levels above him, and listed for the man everything that he, Sam Keenes, could think of that was "absurd and ridiculous" in the division. Sam said it had been one of the great moments in his life. The Vice President listened to the whole thing, Sam said, and ended up explaining to Sam that Taltex was not big enough to hold all the "great talents," so he would understand if Sam felt a need to "expand somewhere else." Sam said they shook hands, and the Vice President wished him the best.

Jesse had resigned, too, from his previous electronic components sales job. We offered him two thousand a year more than what he was making. He got his employer to come up with a two-thousand-dollar raise. Then we upped the offer by another two thousand and told him to take it or leave it. He took it, and called his employer from our office.

John had been living comfortably in retirement until his daughter came down with a severe illness. He did some consulting work that led to nowhere in terms of money. When we gave him the job he was more than grateful. And did he work hard. He came to the office at least one and a half hours before anyone else showed up. Day in and day out. No overtime though—he left promptly at five-thirty, no matter what. At first, we thought he had to tend to his daughter after work. Then one of us ran into him at a Burger King. He was the night shift manager. Sam then gave him a small raise and got him to promise no moonlighting anymore. But he still left at five-thirty. And we never went back to Burger King to check.

John had a way of speaking very even-tempered about everything, and always had a good attitude. We liked spending time with him because he was very funny. He was also a lot more experienced in the electronics business.

When Sam asked him why he'd work himself to death at the Burger King, John gave Sam a boyish smile and said nothing. Sam asked again, and John simply said, "I had more reasons to do it than I had not to do it. So I did it." There was nothing Sam could think of to say to that.

When I resigned as a dog washer at this dog training school in Lubbock, I felt I had saved my own life. I'd worked only three days in that place, and the owner, a middle-aged, bald-headed man dressed in khaki shirt and pants was very happy to have me. His assistant, though, was nothing but trouble. I was asked to wash a great big old St. Bernard the first day. "This will be all you do for the day," the assistant said with a sneer. "We will start you on the regular work tomorrow." It was summer of 1973. I was still forming my opinions about America, with one of them being: "Work is great. People at work are nice people." My experiences at Hong Hong Chinese Restaurant and the Texas Tech University Press as a book binder had seemed beautiful living proofs.

The St. Bernard was too big a job for me. First of all, it weighed as much as I did. Secondly, there was not a dog that hated water more. And thirdly, the assistant never even looked my way, let alone lifting a helping finger, no matter how life-threatening the situation had become. Within two minutes it was quite obvious, to me and the dog, that I was the one getting the wash. The leash only helped the dog jerk me around, so I ended up in the big plastic tub more than him. This, I was sure, was much to the delight of the assistant. Finally, he said, from the side of his mouth, "Go home, then. I'll take care of everything." I was so angry I felt tears coming to my eyes.

The next day, the assignment was to clean about four or five big cages, each containing three German shepherds. All of them growled and barked at me like mad. I tried hard to steady my moves and got most of the dog waste out by a shovel and a bucket of water. In cage No. 3, though, there was a dog with, I swear, eyes that were almost completely red. At first, he threatened me with wild barking, like the others. Then he got closer and actually snapped his jaws shut a couple of times. By the third day, when I was about to enter his cage, I could see he was ready for me. He was off to a corner by himself, not growling or barking with the rest of the gang. But I knew he was going to pounce on me the moment I turned my back to clean up his dirt. He had waited all night. I also knew I had to quit this job even though it paid well.

I marched into the office and found the assistant sitting on a sofa. His girlfriend was next to him.

"I quit," I said, and gave him the bucketful of dirt.

"Yeah?" he said, mockingly.

"Yeah. You do things wrong!" I was angry and wanted him to know my feelings. At the time, this was the best I could do. Then I left in a hurry, forgetting to ask for my three days' pay.

Anyway, the Black Friday started out like any other day. By eight-thirty Mary had made copies of the telexes for everyone and all of us were busy with whatever we were supposed to do. Sally, the Advertising Manager, was looking over the new brochures with Sam in the conference room. John and Jerry were making corrections on the new set of technical manuals and packaging specifications. The office was quiet, even with most of us talking. The soft morning sunshine was quickly retreating from the east side of the office.

When Carolyn called me, it was barely nine-thirty.

One thing Carolyn Coldwell did, often, was go over the heads of people who reported directly to her. She'd talk to anyone in the company, at any time, three or four levels down as she wished, without telling his or her supervisor. Before the meeting or after. Some of the executives were upset at the beginning, more because of their egos than anything else, but as they saw Carolyn get more of Mr. Coldwell's empire in her hands, the same executives only calmed down and pretended it didn't matter. Sam and, for the first two years, Roger knew of every conversation I had with Mr. Coldwell, with or without their presence. Carolyn didn't care much about all this. In a sense we all worked directly for her—the drivers, the secretaries, the lawyers, and the executive vice presidents. In another sense, it would appear all of us were after our boss's job. It was true, one might say, in my case. By the time Carolyn and I finished our conversation, I got Sam's job.

•   •   •

"I think it's time we close it down," Carolyn said, before I was even in a seat.

"What?" I quickly got situated. We were in her private conference room. There were six leather chairs around a nice, smooth marble-top table. A floral arrangement sat on a side stand. Next to it was a small refrigerator from which Carolyn got a soda. She offered me a Coke.

"I've talked to my uncle about this. It has gone on long enough. We either gonna make money or we're shutting it down. It doesn't seem like we're making money, does it?"

"No . . . but I saw Sam's forecast for—"

"My uncle's opinion is about the same. It has dragged on too long." Carolyn took a drink of her soda. She had on a bright yellow sweater and a black-and-green silk scarf. Her eyes were clear, and when she talked, she stared straight at me like a child.

"But . . . but there are ongoing projects, there are people who still owe us money. If we collect, maybe we'll even be profitable this year."

"Exactly. That's why we can't let everybody go. We only want to keep a few who can finish the whole thing for us."

"We have done quite a lot in the past few years. For the long-term business. You might want to think about it. There's been a lot of investment." I had a hard time looking into her eyes.

"Look," Carolyn said. She was getting restless. "Of course there's been a lot of money. That's why we don't want to put in more. I know very little about this kind of business. All I know is, I don't want to pour money on the problems, like my uncle. I want out." Carolyn frowned to let me know the talk was over. She wanted her things done.

176

"What do you think we should do, for the . . . for the shut-down." I was nervous. The fact Sam was not in this discussion began to bother me.

"What do you think we should do, Eric? How many people do you need?" Carolyn's voice had softened.

"What do you mean?"

"How many people do we need besides yourself?" Carolyn said quickly, as if she was already late for another meeting. "We want you to stay. You are bilingual so you can deal with the Chinese, for whatever things we need to deal with them in the future. But we can't just keep only you. If you need more people to help you clean up, we should give you more people. The rest, we'll let them go immediately."

"I see," I said, very much defeated. Carolyn glanced at me, turned away, and waited. For *my* answer. She wanted me to tell her how many people she could safely fire. I was uncomfortable with the pressure. I stared at my ballpoint pen for the longest time. Carolyn started making phone calls. One side of her conference room had tall windows overlooking the traffic on Central Expressway. It was almost eleven; the cars on the highway moved swiftly in both directions. I spent most of the time gazing at the traffic while Carolyn was on the phone.

"Well, Eric, sir, what do you think?" Carolyn smiled. She'd turned to talk to me as soon as she hung up the phone.

"I . . . I think we should keep four or five people."

"No, Eric, no. I tell you what," Carolyn slapped the palm of her hand on the marble top like a man. "We'll let them all go. You keep the secretary, what's her name?"

"Mary."

"Mary. And we will see. Maybe we'll ask one or two of them to

177

come back, if there's a need. In the meantime, we'll keep you and the secretary. Okay?"

"Okay."

"That's it then. Thank you very much." Carolyn picked up a piece of candy from a bowl on the table and plopped it in her mouth.

"Thank you." As I rose to leave the room, I noticed the door was not closed. I could look out, from inside of the conference room, to the big office area, where many men and women in dark suits and dresses worked at their desks. I could also see large paintings hanging on the long walls, right above the heads of these men and women.

"By the way, congratulations," Carolyn said. "I've got the paperwork going. You are now the President of Coldwell Electronics."

"Thank you."

"The Chinese should be thrilled—now that we have made one of their countrymen a president," Carolyn said. "Oh, yeah, I'll call Sam. You take care of the rest."

"Yes, okay," I said. Carolyn picked up the phone again.

When I stepped into the office, Sam was on the phone talking with Carolyn Coldwell. His voice was subdued. I couldn't see his expression because he was facing the wall. He was standing, motionless. In about half a minute, the conversation was over. Sam slammed the phone down. He opened the drawers and put a few things in a big brown envelope. Then he walked right out of the office. He walked past me, Mary, John, and the others, whistling as he moved, never said goodbye to any of us. He only walked, whistled, and left. He looked relaxed, though, and pleasant. And he didn't look back either. The last we saw of him—his back getting smaller in the long corridor of the Coldwell Building.

Sam left at about a quarter past twelve. Half of the people were gone for lunch. I decided, since no one suspected anything yet, to wait until after lunch to break the news. The Personnel Department at Mr. Coldwell's headquarters was standing by. What I needed to do, one by one, was to tell everybody they were fired, and send them all to Personnel. They would then go through an "exit interview." It basically meant turning in the office keys and getting a final check and so forth. For the Personnel people it meant making sure no one, once terminated, could find a single reason to "interface" with the company anymore. Five quick and clean minutes.

So I asked Mary to come along with me to the cafeteria, thinking it would be an excellent time to talk things over with her. We were down there for about an hour, until one-forty. And I ended up telling her a few jokes and nothing about what had happened. What got me started was the young black woman in the cafeteria serving line. She asked me what type of chicken meat I wanted, dark or white. I was absentminded then, and said, "Black, please." And Mary started giggling very loud. So the young woman turned to Mary and said, "What about you, ma'am? Black chicken, too?" After that, Mary was not able to control herself. When we sat down at a table by the mechanical water fountain, I felt much better, and was not of the mind to talk seriously.

One of the jokes I told Mary was from my country. It was about a forty-year-old man who had lived in poverty all his life. Everything he had ever done had failed miserably. One day he decided he'd had enough of bad luck and it was time for a change. So he scraped up all the money to go to a fortune-teller. The fortune-teller took long looks at his palms and said, slowly, "Mister, the first forty years of your life, you definitely lived in poverty."

"That's right!" The forty-year-old man exclaimed, his heart pounding wildly. "But, oh Master, please tell what will be the next forty years of my life. Please!"

The Master took longer looks at the man's palms, stopped to think very seriously. "And the next forty years of your life, sir," the fortune-teller finally said, " . . . the next forty years of your life you'll get used to poverty."

On the way back to the office, Mary and I didn't say much to each other. I had my mind pretty much on what was going to happen next. It was almost two. I had to get everything done by five, the Personnel Director had said. Considering it might take fifteen minutes to talk to one person, I would need a good three hours. I knew I had to begin as soon as I could. But I still waited. I opened a couple of file folders on my desk and stared at them. I thought of calling Mr. Coldwell directly, to see if this was what he really meant to do—firing a bunch of people just like that. It was always possible that I could happen to say something that might change his mind. I quickly forgot the idea though, knowing how unlikely that I could get him on the line, and how *dumb* it would be for me to bypass Carolyn Coldwell. I still felt like talking to someone. I needed the heavy feelings out of my system, for one thing. And I needed a suggestion or two about what to say to my people, how I might make the whole thing sound more *justified*, if at all possible, and not as cold. I picked up the phone, but could think of no one to call. I closed and straightened my folders. An old memorandum slipped out from one of the folders. I picked it up, read it, and placed it back carefully. Then I reached for the phone again, and—I don't know why I did this—dialed Roger Holton's home number. Roger of all people. I must have felt Roger *owed* me; after all, the wonderful and glorious Coldwell Electronics International, Inc., was his invention.

"Hello." The phone was answered on the first ring. It was Roger.

"Roger . . . " I was surprised to hear his voice. Usually, when I'd called before, there had been a recorded message giving his office number. "How are you, Roger? This is Eric. Eric Chung."

"Oh, hi, Eric . . . " Roger sounded surprised but glad. "Long time no see! What do you know—a voice from the past!" He was almost yelling on the phone. "What's going on, my man?"

"Nothing . . . nothing much here. How *are* you? Everything all right with you? I haven't heard from you for so long . . . for a couple of years at least," I said.

"Well," Roger sighed. "I'm doing as much as I can not to overcommit myself. Too many irons in the fire is not necessarily good, you know. I'm trying to give quality time to all my projects —and *that* is getting hard to find nowadays. There are just too many things going on."

"You are doing great then," I said, trying to sound convinced. "I am glad . . . for you."

"Well, you live and learn. One thing I learned, from my Coldwell days, was that you don't make offers. You wait for people to ask, then you make offers. Coldwell never appreciated what he got from me because he didn't have to ask . . . But that's all in the past. How's Coldwell Electronics, by the way? You guys making money yet? Is Sam still holding up okay?"

"Everything's still pretty much the same, Roger. We are trying hard." I'd changed my mind about telling Roger what was going on. My gloom and doom seemed totally out of place. "Sam is hanging on, but, you know how it is, most things are not in his control."

"Of course not. Someone must set the Chinese straight, or Coldwell's not gonna see a cent out of this deal. Well . . . " Roger sighed again, "if there's anything I can do—I know what you are going through—like giving Coldwell Electronics some of my consulting time or something, just let me know. I know it's tough. And the Chinese are going to make it tougher. Believe me."

"Things are so complicated I doubt anybody can help—"

"Speaking of the Chinese," Roger interrupted, "I am very close to putting together a project for a group of major investors. It's about copper, that's all I can tell you now. But I'd like to keep in touch, because we are involving China at the highest level. I'm sure you know who in China I'm talking about." Roger waited, as if deciding whether to tell me more. "We are going at this extra cautiously. If there's any mess-up at all, any leak or something, the consequences are too serious to think about."

"Sounds exciting. Sounds like a huge project," I said. "Are you going to China soon—"

"I am telling you this, Eric," Roger interrupted me again, "so that you know we may have, or I may have, ways to help you." Roger sounded enthusiastic as ever, and I felt I was now in a more positive mood. You had to be positive when talking to Roger. He wouldn't have it otherwise.

"It's very nice to know you are doing well, Roger." I spoke from my heart. "It's nice to know you are doing well." Roger then gave me three numbers where he could be reached at different times. He was at home all afternoons. In the mornings, his projects kept him "shuttling between two offices." I wrote the phone numbers down on a small piece of paper.

"Keep charging. Stay on the pills," Roger joked. Then he hung up the phone. Good old Roger.

The conversation with Roger had taken another twenty minutes. I had no time left. I called Mary into my office and asked her to send out telegrams for those who were out on the road and on vacation. The telegrams were to read:

Dear (name): Please be advised that major restructuring of Coldwell Electronics International, Inc., will require the company to terminate your employment. Please contact the office as soon as possible to commence proper exit procedures. With deep regret, Coldwell Electronics International, Inc.

For the twelve people in the office, the speech I had for them was the one I have told you.

I began calling each person into my office at about two-thirty. I started with John because I felt it would be difficult for me to give him the news. He was also the one I felt was most capable of keeping calm about it. Once I started, things went on rather quickly:

FIRED 2:43 P.M.   John Drew, Chief Engineer

FIRED 2:50 P.M.   Jesse Halstead, Vice President, Marketing

FIRED 3:02 P.M.   Sandy Fowler, Accounting Clerk

FIRED 3:09 P.M.   Sally Nuber, Advertising Manager

FIRED 3:17 P.M.   Oliver Hall, Project Engineer

FIRED 3:24 P.M.   Linda Freeman, Accounting Manager

FIRED 3:33 P.M.	Jerry Howard, Project Engineer
FIRED 3:42 P.M.	Jean Barta, Accounting Secretary
FIRED 3:55 P.M.	Robert Turner, Sales Engineer

At about 4:00 P.M., Mary came and interrupted my conversation with Robert Turner and told me all the telegrams had been sent out. She threw the sheet of original text back on my desk.

"All done," she said. There was no expression whatsoever on her face. I didn't thank her either.

Robert Turner could not believe what he'd heard. He'd worked under Sam at Taltex for six years. It had taken Sam over two years to get him to leave Taltex. This was only his fourth month at Coldwell Electronics International, Inc.

FIRED BY TELEGRAMS 4:01 P.M.	Fred Hodel (traveling), Sales Manager Mark Johnson (traveling), Sales Manager Ross Miller (traveling), Sales Manager Linda Broderick (on vacation), Receptionist Robert Wadin (on vacation), Market Analyst
FIRED 4:05 P.M.	Harry Tucker, Project Manager
FIRED 4:15 P.M.	Hank Lorenzo, Engineering Technician

| FIRED 4:27 P.M. | Sherry Silberner, Market Analyst |
| FIRED 4:38 P.M. | Lou Grossman, Engineering Technician |

I stayed in my office until about five-thirty to fill out all the forms for the personnel people. When I was through, I noticed the quietness of the office. The paper I threw in the wastebasket made such a noise that it startled me. I stood up and looked around in my office for a while before I walked out. Mary was at her desk. It looked kind of odd with her sitting by herself in the middle of a big office area. Most of the desks were clean and neat with the exception of a few open drawers. Oliver had left a picture in a small brass frame of him and his wife. There were thick files piled up on John's desk—important specification sheets he wanted us to be able to find quickly. I assumed Mary had cried, so I didn't look at her for a while. When I went up to her desk, I saw her face darkened by shadows cast by the afternoon sunlight, now coming in from the other side of the office. She was reading some telexes and mail that had come in sometime during late afternoon. I stood in front of her and flipped through the letters. I said to her, "Well, it's all done. Just you and me left, Mary."

"Yeah," Mary said. She didn't raise her head. I walked out of the office and went home. 5:57 P.M.

18. Picnic Weather

WHEN I GOT TO MY APARTMENT, the television was still on. This was not the first time I'd forgotten to turn it off in the morning before leaving. All the lights and everything else were off, though, including the air conditioner. A movie was going on that was making loud noises. A man and a woman were hiding behind a big van in the movie. They were being shot at by another man from across the street. The man with a shotgun had on a cowboy hat. Each time there was a gunshot, the woman screamed. I went to the refrigerator and took out a couple of TV dinners for the microwave. When I sat down, the cowboy had gotten hold of the man and had thrown him down on the ground. The woman kept screaming. I felt like turning the TV off because it was getting on my nerves. But I decided to wait until my dinner was ready. I didn't want to have the quietness until I had something to do, like eating. The cowboy was really letting the man have it with his punches. He was sitting on top of the man, who was probably already half dead, and was whacking away with left and right punches at the poor man's head. The woman threw herself a couple of times on the cowboy and was thrown back. There was now the sound of punches and the woman was wailing something to the cowboy. The microwave stopped with a ding, so I went up to get the food. When I returned, I turned off the TV.

I ate in the small and now very quiet living room of my apartment. All the noises of the cowboy and the woman were gone just like that. With one push of the button. A while ago, they'd been real. They'd interested me, and bothered the heck out of me at the same time. But they were gone now. Out of my life, so I could have dinner.

And the quietness began to make me sick about what had happened in the office. Everybody was gone, too, at Coldwell Electronics International, Inc. I would not see or hear from them anymore. That hit me real hard. It's like Carolyn and Mr. Coldwell pushed the button, I thought, and the whole crew's gone like magic. Like the cowboy and the man and the woman. All gone. A minute ago they'd been all there, you could almost have touched the blood coming out the man's mouth. But no matter. Now they were clearly gone.

I was definitely getting depressed about what I was thinking. I finished only half of the dinner. Then I sat around and drank the Coke for a while, and put on a record. But I quickly got bored at that, too, and began pacing around in the apartment. Finally, I sat down and turned on the TV again. The same movie was still going on. This time the man was holding the guns, one in each hand, and was walking slowly toward the cowboy, now backed into a corner. The woman was still there, in a nice-looking dress. There was another man that looked like a judge or a banker or something. The man stopped and began shooting at the cowboy's arms and legs. With each shot, blood came out of a new spot from his arms or legs. The cowboy groaned with great pain, and he looked at the man like he was begging for life. Then the woman started screaming again. That got me laughing very hard, thinking to myself, "Which side is she on anyway?" I turned off the TV. And a few minutes later I turned it on again. Then I turned it off and on a few more times, quickly. The movie came in and out like a neon sign. Then I threw away the remote control.

A wave of angry feeling started to rise in me as I was cleaning things up in the kitchen. I remembered what Carolyn Coldwell had said about letting everyone go and "maybe" asking one or two to come back, "if there was a need." I got angry at that for a while, then I got angrier at everybody who had left. Sam, Sally, Jerry, John, Oliver, Jesse. Everybody. None of them had put up a fight, I thought. They'd all let Carolyn—and me—wipe them off the book just like that. One push of the button. I didn't know what Sam had said to Carolyn on the phone, if anything at all. All twelve were nothing but wimps when I talked to them. No one had gotten ugly. No one really had said anything. No one had asked a question either, except John. And all he'd wanted to know was if I knew of someone who was hiring. It was not going to be easy for him, he said, because of his age, and he needed a job as much as anybody. I thought of how quiet everybody had been when they were told, and how they all went out of my office like they didn't belong. I thought of Oliver giving me a number to call, just in case. I was so angry I was beginning to hear my heart pound.

I thought the least they could have done was to raise a point or two. Like what was wrong with working their hearts out doing what they'd been told to do? You could perhaps get some "outrage" out of it or something. And make the whole thing sound like another example of Coldwell's "ruthlessness." Then I thought about how little justice there was, since none of the people fired, including Sam, had had anything to do with the China idea in the first place. I had, in a way, and I'd got to stay. All they had been doing was working their best for a bad idea. That's all.

I also wondered why Carolyn had not mentioned the possibilities of putting some in the other Coldwell companies. She was not obligated, of course, but these people were good, dedicated workers, anybody could see that.

By about ten-thirty I was developing a splitting headache. I took a couple of aspirin and began pacing the apartment again. I heard someone playing a guitar outside of the apartment. I listened to it for a while and let it make me feel drowsy. I turned on the TV again; this time I saw the weatherman joking with the anchorwoman and the sportsman. They went back and forth at each other and ended up laughing loudly together. Then the weatherman, with his large red bow tie, began to tell the weather for the next day. There were charts, maps, and satellite pictures and all, which he had to point to. Basically, though, he was saying the weather was going to be very nice and sunny. "Picnic weather," he said. In the end, before the commercial, he summed it all up: "In any case, it will be a wonderful day tomorrow." He smiled big and pointed at me, and I guess millions of others. "Enjoy it," he said.

I went to sleep with my work clothes on. I also left the TV on all night.

19. Our Mutual Business

I THINK YOU CAN PRETTY MUCH figure out what has happened since Black Friday, if I haven't already told more than you ever wanted to know. You might want to ask whether it has ever occurred to me that I should get on with it, like looking for a new job or something, instead of sitting around and feeling sorry for myself. It has. But it doesn't change much. I just don't get too excited about a new job, yet. I think maybe I need more time. Maybe what I need is for Carolyn Coldwell to go ahead and fire me. Push the button. Give me the ax. Then I'd better think of something quick. I'd better.

I must say I am somewhat grateful that the paychecks are still coming in. But they give you a strange feeling, these paychecks, like you came out without a scratch from a battlefield where everybody else died. As if there was a scheme or something. Luckily, I don't let it bother me too much. You've got to learn to deal with this "feeling" stuff, or you don't get very far at all. With anything. Carolyn Coldwell is a perfect example. She's trained to stay cool. In my opinion, she's geared for the greatest success. The *Morning News* did an article a few weeks back about her. She was called "heir apparent," by the *News*, to Mr. Coldwell's empire. The

News said she was "quick-witted, good-humored" and could "make direct, simple, and rational decisions amid complex business situations." Mr. Coldwell was called a "great visionary" in the article.

I also need to tell you, in all fairness, that Carolyn Coldwell did sort of offer me another job. It was about two weeks before we were moved down here. She and I were having one of our biweekly meetings on how the "clean-up" process at Coldwell Electronics International, Inc., was going. These meetings were usually short and sweet, because there were not too many new things to say. Carolyn Coldwell had said the Chinese had "behaved extremely well" since the Black Friday. Mr. Yeh of the Planning Division had been sending monthly "Factory Reports" to show how many more of his products were about to become "goods of world standard." Madame Li had written a formal letter to Carolyn, in both English and Chinese versions, praising Carolyn Coldwell as a "leader of wisdom," calling the Black Friday a "transition toward success." In the same letter Madame Li had also reminded Carolyn Coldwell that "long-term faith" was necessary for building "big businesses."

To me, Madame Li had been a lot more direct. She had sent me a couple of short sentences by telex:

ATTENTION: Eric Chung
I have heard about the misfortune. Is Mr. Coldwell going to continue our mutual business?
BEST REGARDS, Madame Li

I had not responded to the telex. Carolyn Coldwell, on the other hand, had written back in an equally formal letter, inviting Madame Li to take "immediate measures" to make things right. The Chinese version of this letter was prepared by me.

Anyway, I was halfway into my report in the biweekly meeting, when Carolyn Coldwell interrupted me, like she'd always done when something different popped up in her mind.

"By the way, you probably know from the newspaper we are creating a new hotel company."

"Yes." I had, and still have, a lot of time to read newspapers. What Carolyn and Mr. Coldwell were doing, according to the story, was to get rid of the hotel management company that had been running all their hotels and start their own. It was going to be a new hotel chain. Like Hilton or Marriott.

"There's going to be some jobs opening up," Carolyn said thoughtfully. "You might want to see how you can fit in."

"Yes, ma'am." I said. Then I went into my report.

Carolyn Coldwell has not mentioned the hotel job since. Not that she has changed her mind. If I had gotten more aggressive about it and put together a fancy "proposal" to tell her how my "past training" and "academic background" had made me the "ideal candidate" for a "senior management position" in a "hotel-related industry," I'd probably have the job all wrapped up by now. Maybe the General Manager of a 1200-room hotel. Maybe the Regional Food and Beverage Director or something. Who knows. But I haven't got my mind into it yet. I don't mean to say I haven't thought about it at all, I have. After the meeting, when I was on the way back to our empty office, I thought a lot about it. I also wanted to tell Mary, thinking she might be affected, too. As I was stepping into our office area, Mary beat me with her news first.

"Sam's got a job," she said. She had on a bright flowery dress and looked cheerful.

"Oh, yeah? Where?" I asked.

"Boston. He is going to be the Vice President of Sales for DCC Industries."

"Wow."

"Yeah. I've just heard," Mary said. She looked like a little girl who just came in first in a school race or something.

"Okay. Now he's a fish in a bigger pond."

"What?" Mary looked at me suspiciously. She must have thought I was going to start my jokes again.

"Nothing."

"I'm going to check the mail," she said.

"Go ahead," I nodded, and as she was leaving, I said to her back, "and *my* water is getting lower and lower."

While Mary was gone, Roger called to see if Coldwell Electronics International, Inc., was ready to "retain" him on a "problem-solving/consulting basis."

"Let me call you back, Roger," I told him. "You have caught me at a bad time."

Anyway, I didn't tell Mary about the hotel thing when she returned. But I kept thinking about it for a while. All this probably wouldn't make any difference now. But I need to tell you, in all fairness to Carolyn Coldwell.

EPILOGUE

IN ALL FAIRNESS, TOO, what I have now is not entirely bad. For one thing, there's a world of time to *calm down* after all that has occurred. Unlimited peace and quiet, if you will. About the only way I can be disturbed is by my own thoughts. And I don't need to do much thinking either, not when nothing important is likely to happen. I only think about very few things nowadays, and not too much on any of them. Granted, there are still the *feelings* in me. They are unavoidable, I guess. But as long as I am not agitated much by them, they'll quietly pass.

All this is generally good, I suppose, for my mind.

A big thing I think about is writing a letter to Petrochem—to Mr. Lambert, the company chairman. Of the thousands of stories I've read in the *Morning News*, one the other day was about Petrochem. Here is part of it:

PETROCHEM EARNS $62 MILLION

By Jim Dodge
  Staff Writer of The News

Petrochem Inc., earned $62 million in the second quarter, an indication that the world market for petroleum products is rebounding, company Chairman, Jeff Lambert, said.

The earnings of 56 cents a share came on sales of $3.21 billion. During the same period a year ago, Petrochem lost $12.3 million or 16 cents per share on revenue of $1.9 billion.

Lambert said in a press conference the company's second-quarter shipments "outpaced the growth of the world market." If world petroleum market conditions continue to improve, then the company's growth "could be at a somewhat higher rate than the 11 percent we projected at the stockholder's meeting in April," he said.

The company also said it plans a "moderate" increase in capital spending. . . .

Anyway, the article went on for much, much longer. It didn't say anything about the "diversification efforts" this Lambert fellow had started when they fired Victor, though. Neither did the company, or Lambert, say anything about what they would do now with the one thousand nine hundred and ninety-nine they had fired along with Victor. It was "poor business conditions" then—I still have a copy of the paper. Now they say nothing.

I could be totally wrong, but the way I feel about it, Jeff Lambert owes Victor an apology. A big one. And I wonder what he would say if I told him so.

Another thing I think about is learning more English. I need to get *urgent* about this. More grammar, more vocabulary, more sports, more jokes, more everything. I bet things would get easier for me, as a result. I must know better and speak better in this society. Simple as that. "Jump into the melting pot," like Victor always said. Americanize. And Victor was right about this.

I have already picked out a few more words to practice on. "Nefarious," "vicissitudes," and several more.

And, also, I think about what I should say to Carolyn Coldwell. She'll want to talk. As soon as she sees me, still drawing a salary, on her financial reports. As soon as she realizes there's nothing left for me to do. The talk will be either about my "termination," in which case I plan to simply say a nice goodbye, or—an outside chance—a "new position" with a Coldwell hotel or whatever. I can't think of anything thing else she might want to talk to me about. I can't imagine why she wouldn't want this talk *soon*, like first thing next week.

I am just not sure about staying with Carolyn Coldwell anymore. I think I want something "less volatile," if you will. Then, in all fairness again, even with a totally different job, I could still end up with the same miseries, say another six years down the road. There's no guarantee things are going to be different somewhere else. Chances are good that they *aren't*. History is made of vicious cycles, if you ask me. *Nefarious* cycles?

Another of the things I am currently thinking about is how to keep my father from coming here for a while. Recently my father has been writing more and more about "taking it easy" in the United States. "After evaluations, I feel I can spend the rest of my life with serenity and good health in *your* America"—so went one of his letters. Others were more or less the same. I frankly do not think he should come, not to *my* America anyway. I have not written my father one negative thing about here. Not one in fifteen years. No George's or my being robbed in Lubbock. No Roger's being fired. No Victor's suicide. No Black Friday. Nothing even close. You'd think I live in a paradise if you read those wonderful letters of mine. Or at least in a place unmistakably a thousand times better than our "dogs eat dogs" island. I know I owe my father some explaining. And I know I shouldn't simply say America is really worse than he thinks. That would be irresponsible. Probably not truthful, either. But I have a hard time coming up with the *right* things to say.

The fact is I don't really have a good idea, yet, about America. I can *talk* about it, like any other immigrant, but I don't *know* it. Not much anyway. I might need a couple more years. Given enough time, people can generally form their views about America. My father did, and he has never been here. It's just taking me much longer.

I came to Dallas for the first time about ten years ago when I was to interview with Taltex—not knowing I was making my own "historical move." I remember the seven-hour drive from Lubbock well. I took off about two in the afternoon on a Thursday with driving directions provided by my prospective boss, the Systems Programming Manager, who had said his department was "more than willing" to talk to me, but could not provide "travel allowances." At the time I considered his attitude to be *unfriendly* and a sore reminder of the much better deal Victor had gotten from Petrochem.

The directions had come with good details. I passed towns like Snyder, Sweetwater, Abilene, and Cisco as I had expected. These towns were small and unimportant in my mind, but they were the only things to see along the way, other than George's "good sunset" —and three hours straight of *that* can make you tired. The road was so straight and the land so empty that you'd think the car had not moved an inch for hours.

Anyway, everything went beautifully as planned until I got lost on the highway coming into Dallas. Too many road signs and intersections suddenly came up—driving in Lubbock had never been so complicated. I missed an exit on I-20 and ended up driving up and down on Loop 12 where I didn't belong. I drove aimlessly and finally headed toward a group of tall buildings which I could see from miles away, hoping to find the Taltex building somehow. And also I wanted to see Dallas better. The tall buildings with tiny dots of lights made quite a scenic skyline in the night. I turned into the downtown area at about ten and spent a good thirty minutes circling the streets. I was impressed with all the buildings. It was hard to decide whether Taltex was anywhere close. I couldn't ask people either, there was virtually no one on the streets. At this time far away in my home city, I thought to myself, people would be standing on each other in downtown. And we didn't have tall buildings.

I finally stopped the car in front of a very handsome granite building, thinking it was a good place to stretch my legs and to look around. I was now less concerned about finding Taltex and more excited about being in the heart of a world-class "metropolis," the first in my life. I walked on the sidewalk and breathed the air.

The granite building, which I was looking at, was brightened by many floodlights from the ground. It reminded me of the American movies I had seen back home. The other buildings close by were also tall and good-looking. The idea of living and working in this city was becoming very appealing. I paced on the sidewalk and saw a man and a woman walk towards me. The woman, in a bright red low-cut dress, was obviously a prostitute. The man waved at me but I ignored him. The woman said, "Don't go home too late, hon," as they passed me.

I walked back to my car, and before opening the car door, I turned toward the big granite building and said, under my breath, "Hello, Dellas, here I come." That's what I said. "Dellas, here I come." I said it a couple of times.